F
Patten, Lewis B.
The hide hunters

The Hide Hunters

The Hide Hunters

Lewis B. Patten

THORNDIKE
CHIVERS

This Large Print edition is published by Thorndike Press®, Waterville, Maine USA and by BBC Audiobooks Ltd, Bath, England.

Published in 2006 in the U.S. by arrangement with Golden West Literary Agency.

Published in 2006 in the U.K. by arrangement with Golden West Literary Agency.

U.S. Hardcover 0-7862-8527-3   (Western)
U.K. Hardcover 10: 1 405 63745 5   (Chivers Large Print)
U.K. Hardcover 13: 978 1 405 63745 9
U.K. Softcover 10: 1 405 63746 3   (Camden Large Print)
U.K. Softcover 13: 978 1 405 63746 6

The text of this Large Print edition is unabridged.
Other aspects of the book may vary from the original edition.

Set in 16 pt. Plantin by Carleen Stearns.

Printed in the United States on permanent paper.

British Library Cataloguing-in-Publication Data available

Library of Congress Cataloging-in-Publication Data

Patten, Lewis B.
    The hide hunters / by Lewis B. Patten.
        p. cm. — (Thorndike Press large print westerns)
    ISBN 0-7862-8527-3 (lg. print : hc : alk. paper)
        1. Hunters — Fiction.   2. Large type books.   I. Title.
    II. Thorndike Press large print Western series.
    PS3566.A79H53 2006
    813'.54—dc22   2006001544

The Hide Hunters

Chapter 1

Off and on all morning I had spotted small
bunches of cattle in the distance, so I knew
there had to be a ranch house someplace
close. As I rounded a bend in the dry watercourse I was following I saw it finally, sitting
squat, ugly, and barren against the dry,
brown hillside beyond.

My name is Jess Burdett. I'm pretty solid
and I've always been strong enough for
whatever had to be done. My hair is graying
a little over my ears. I'm six feet two inches
tall and I weigh two hundred and fifteen
pounds — when I'm eating regular.

I halted my horse about a hundred yards
away and stared at the ranch house, looking
for signs of life. Like most buildings in this
part of the country it was built of adobe
bricks, with the poles that formed the roof
extending out far enough in front to make a
wide, shaded gallery. In back there was an
outhouse, an adobe shed, and a small corral,
also built out of adobe brick. As I watched, a
horse got up inside the corral, shook the
dust from himself, and then stood there

staring curiously at me.

The horse told me the place was inhabited. I was still a little edgy, though, as I rode closer. This was Comanche and Kiowa country, and those two tribes weren't exactly happy about the white men slaughtering buffalo south of the Arkansas. That section had been set aside permanently as their hunting grounds by the Medicine Lodge Treaty seven years before. Trouble was, north of the Arkansas the buffalo were getting scarce.

A couple of white chickens came from behind the house. They paid no attention to me and went on scratching unconcernedly.

Looking beyond the house, I saw a lone figure trudging northward on foot. At this distance it was hard to be sure, but it looked like a woman. I began to get pretty puzzled, because this was strange. Why would a woman who lived here walk when there was a horse standing in the corral?

Still about fifty feet away I yelled, "Hey! Anybody home?"

I got no answer and nothing stirred. An unpleasant little chill started at the base of my neck. I stayed put and stared around at the hillsides and horizons but I didn't see anything. Finally, I got down off my horse

8

and, drawing my revolver, approached the house.

I knocked. Getting no answer, I opened the stout plank door, which had a latch-string hanging out. No one was inside. The place had an earthen floor, packed and neatly swept. The sheet-iron stove in the corner was slightly warm, a sure sign it had been used this morning. There wasn't much furniture, just a long, rough table with a bench on either side of it.

I crossed the room to a curtain of sewed-together pieces of homespun material which partitioned off the far end of the room. Behind it there was a bed, neatly made. But no one was there.

When I'd first seen this house in the distance, I'd hoped maybe I could get myself a home-cooked meal. I was disappointed that I wasn't going to. I went outside again, still puzzled by that trudging figure in the distance.

For a moment I stood there in the cool shade of the gallery. Then I walked to my horse, mounted, and headed north again.

Three quarters of a mile from the house I overtook the woman. She swung around quickly when she heard my horse's hoofs. She was carrying an old, rusty double-barreled shotgun. She raised it and pointed it at me.

I was shocked by the way her face looked. Both of her eyes were swelled nearly shut, and black. There was a large bruise on her cheekbone and another on her jaw. Her mouth was smashed, scabbed, and swollen.

Her eyes, almost lost in the swelling flesh around them, were dark. They looked at me with unmistakable dislike, but I thought I saw something else in them too — shame that I had seen her that way.

I stopped my horse, nervous because of that shotgun pointing at me. I fumbled around for something to say and finally got out, "Ma'am, this is sure no place for a woman to be walkin' all by herself."

She said, "That is no concern of yours. What do you want?" Her voice was low and I thought it might have sounded pleasant if it hadn't been so full of hostility.

I said, "I don't want nothing, ma'am. It just looked like maybe *you* might." I saw that she had a tied-at-the-corners blanket thrown over her shoulder, lumpy with the things she was carrying. I figured she had been badly beaten by her husband and was leaving him. But she wasn't being very practical. It was a hundred and fifty miles to Dodge, which was the nearest sizable settlement. She wouldn't make it on foot and alone.

I said, "He's going to catch you, ma'am. You should have taken that horse in the corral."

Her voice was pretty sharp. "I brought nothing to him and I will take nothing away."

I said, "That's a fine sentiment, but it don't make much sense. A man that'll beat a woman like he beat you ain't going to let her run away from him. He'll come after you and he'll catch you and take you back. Likely he'll beat you worse for trying to run away."

Her eyes looked at me steadily and they didn't seem to be afraid. "He will not touch me when he understands that I will shoot."

I wasn't getting anyplace with her, likely because she was so upset. I figured maybe if I talked to her about it for a while she'd calm down and go back home. I asked, "Has he beat you before? Or is this the first time?"

"I do not wish to discuss it with you. It is a private matter between my husband and myself."

I said, "It ain't private any more." I'd been brought into it just by being here. She didn't want to listen to reason and that irritated me. Finally I said, "You know damn well I can't just leave you here. Comanches would love to find a white woman out here all by

11

herself. And even if they don't find you, you'll never make it all the way to Dodge. It's a hundred and fifty miles. No woman could walk that far."

"How would you expect me to go?" she asked. "Fly?"

In spite of how mad I was, I couldn't help grinning when she said that. She saw the grin and said angrily, "Just go on where you were going and let me alone. I do not need your help."

I looked back toward the ranch house, half expecting to see her husband coming after her. I sure didn't want to get caught in the middle of a family quarrel. That was one of the worst things a man could do. But I didn't see how I could just ride away and leave her here, knowing what she meant to do. I asked, "How long do you figure it will be before your husband comes after you?"

"It will be several days. He has ridden to the Butterworths', on Plum Creek, sixty miles east of here."

"He just went off and left you alone?"

"What else should he do?" she said. "Mr. Butterworth has nearly fifty head of cattle that belong to my husband. They drifted south last winter and were dropped off at Butterworth's by the crew of a trail herd passing through."

"What about that horse in the corral?"

"He has water and enough hay to last until my husband gets back."

I suddenly knew what I'd have to do. Disgustedly I said, "All right. Come on and I'll lift you up."

She just stared at me. She didn't move. "I have no intention of riding anyplace with you, Mr. . . ." She stopped because she didn't know my name. I said, "Burdett. Jess Burdett."

"I have no intention of riding with you, Mr. Burdett. Just go on about your business and leave me to mine."

I said irritably, "By God, you're the stubbornest damn woman I ever saw! What do I have to do, get down and beg?"

"Please do not take the name of the Lord in vain, Mr. Burdett," she said, as if I was a schoolboy and she was my teacher.

I kind of felt like laughing, but I was too damn mad to laugh. I was trying to tell myself that maybe she would be all right. She was tough and self-sufficient, and she seemed used to being alone. She wasn't afraid, or if she was, it didn't show. I figured that in two or three days the wind would have scoured her footprints from the ground. Her husband would have a hard time following her unless he knew which way she'd gone.

13

But I couldn't convince myself. She was heading straight into the Comanche and Kiowa hunting grounds. If they found her, the beating her husband had given her would seem like nothing at all. I said "Damnit to hell, I can't leave you!"

She fixed me with her stare, silently scolding me for the language I had used. Finally she said firmly, "You have no choice, Mr. Burdett. I refuse to ride with you."

I was clear out of patience now. I got off my horse. I'd been put into a hell of a position. I couldn't leave her. If I did, I'd be responsible for whatever happened to her. I couldn't seem to talk her into going along with me of her own free will. That only left me one choice. I'd have to take her by force, and besides probably hurting her, doing that would put me squarely in the wrong, with her, with her husband, and with the law — if we ever got to a place where there was some law.

I was scared of that shotgun but I couldn't let her know. I walked toward her slow and easy, and as I walked I said, as persuasively as I could, "Lady, I can't leave you here, so if you ain't going with me of your own free will, I reckon I'll just have to take you whether you like it or not."

The gun muzzle wavered and I damn near

stopped. I could feel the clammy sweat in my armpits and down my back. Her voice came out, shriller than before, "Stop right where you are! If you don't, I'll shoot!"

I didn't slow down one damn bit. I knew I was a fool, because any woman with a gun is dangerous, and this one had been beaten and was desperate. Her voice when it came again was almost a scream. "I'll shoot!"

My belly was only a foot from the shaking muzzle of her gun when I stopped. I said, "Ma'am, I guess you'll just have to shoot. Because I ain't going to leave you here."

She didn't shoot, but neither did she lower the gun. I said, "Ma'am, you got to fish or cut bait." I looked straight at her and it was her that looked away.

Her shoulders slumped and the gun muzzle sagged until it was pointing at the ground. "I can't shoot you."

I said, "Likely you couldn't shoot your husband, either, ma'am."

She looked up at me, something desperate in her eyes. "I suppose not. But I can't go back. I won't go back!"

"No need to. Just let me hoist you up on my horse." I took her blanket-wrapped possessions and her gun. I unloaded the gun and tied it and the bundle behind the saddle, rearranging my blanket roll and tying

15

everything so she'd have a place to sit. I mounted and reached down. I lifted her and sat her down behind me on the horse's rump. I was surprised at how light she was. Maybe the determination and strength in her had made her seem bigger. The horse turned his head, rolled his eyes, and laid back his ears. I thought, God, I hope he ain't going to pick now to buck. He didn't and I turned him north. I said, "You can hold onto me if you want."

I kept thinking about how light she'd been, and how soft. I wondered what she'd look like without those bruises on her face. I made myself think about something else because those kinds of thoughts were no good. I had plenty of trouble without asking for any more. Her husband was eventually going to come home. When he found her gone, he'd come after her. Wind wasn't going to wipe out my horse's tracks the way it would have wiped out the prints of her little feet.

I couldn't go on calling her ma'am, and besides, I was curious. I asked, "What's your name, ma'am?"

"It is Mrs. Clinger. Edith Clinger. My husband's name is Jake."

I said, "Mrs. Clinger, when you get to Dodge, you'll have the protection of the law.

16

Your husband won't be able to force you to go back with him. If he lays a hand on you, you can have him thrown in jail."

She didn't say anything and I didn't look around. She had to be hurting from the motion of the horse because it wasn't likely her husband's blows had been confined to her face. She didn't complain, though, so I kept pushing the horse all I could. The best way to keep from tangling with her husband was to get her to Dodge before he caught up with us.

Twice, going up a hill, she put her arms around my waist, holding on so that she wouldn't slide off the horse's rump. I made out like I didn't notice, but I did. And I felt myself getting madder at her husband for what he'd done to her.

It was almost mid-afternoon before either of us said anything more. Then Mrs. Clinger asked, "What about yourself, Mr. Burdett? What are you doing way out here?"

I didn't answer right away. I didn't much like what I was going to do, but finally I said, "I'm going to hunt buffalo."

Her silence seemed to me like she was condemning me. I said defensively, "Somebody's going to do it whether I do or not. Hell ma'am, I'd just as well have some of that easy money as anybody else. It's the

17

only way I'm ever going to get a stake. I been working for somebody else all my life, and all I got to show for it is this horse and saddle and the clothes on my back. I'm past forty, Mrs. Clinger. I'm past forty and it's time I had a family and a place of my own."

"There is nothing wrong with that, Mr. Burdett."

"No. It's just that I ain't proud that I'm goin' to kill buffalo to get what I want. Indians live off the buffalo. But, with me or without me, all the buffalo are going to get wiped out."

"Most people out here hate the Indians so much they want to see them die. My husband does."

That was true, but not with me. I said, "I guess if they've hurt you it's natural to hate them and want them dead. They never hurt me, so I got nothing to hate them for."

After that, neither of us said anything for the rest of the day. I kept going until well after dark, wanting to put as much distance between us and her husband as I could. When I did stop, I lifted her down, then unsaddled and picketed my horse so he could graze.

I didn't know if there were Indians around, so I cautioned her not to build a fire. We ate cold jerky from my saddlebags and biscuits and dried apples from the bundle she'd brought along. I had a canteen of water and so did she.

Afterward, I laid down about fifty feet away from her and wrapped myself up in my blankets. I noticed she kept her shotgun right close.

She didn't trust me, and I guessed I couldn't blame her much for that. With a husband like hers, she didn't have much reason to trust any man.

Chapter 2

We were up before the sky was light. It was June but the air was chill. I saddled up and we rode out, satisfying our hunger by chewing a little jerky as we rode. Though my horse seemed rested and had eaten all the grass within the radius of his picket rope, I knew that, sooner or later, carrying double would tell on him.

Edith Clinger was stiff and had limped painfully when she walked earlier. Occasionally I would hear a sharply in-drawn breath behind me as the horse went down into a gully or climbed out of one, but she did not complain.

We didn't talk very much. I wasn't much of a hand for small talk and apparently neither was she. If we had something to say, we said it. Otherwise we said nothing at all.

I had to admire that in a woman. Too many of them talk continuously without saying anything. Mrs. Clinger also seemed a little more comfortable with me today. I hadn't threatened her, so far, and maybe she'd decided I wasn't going to.

We stopped at noon, more to rest my horse than to rest ourselves. I picketed him after he had drunk his fill from a nearly dry stream, and we sat down in the shade of a big red sandstone rock.

I'd seen signs of Indians all morning, but I hadn't mentioned it to her. All the signs had been old, a week or more, so there didn't seem to be anything to worry about just yet. The trouble was, all the trails had been heading north. There must be hundreds of Indians ahead of us.

I went to sleep while Edith Clinger watched. When I woke up, I watched while she slept. It was mid-afternoon before we rode out again.

I stayed in the low ground, gullies, stream-beds, and natural valleys as much as possible, because I knew that when you travel the high ground you can be seen for miles. Maybe we'd come on some Indians and be surprised, but at least we wouldn't advertise our presence here.

I halted early, long before it got dark. Again we rested and again I picketed my horse. As soon as it was full dark, we rode out again. I had decided that from now on we'd travel at night and sleep during the day. In Indian country it's the only sensible thing to do.

All night we rode. I guided myself by the North Star, which I'd learned to recognize while I was still a boy. We stopped once for half an hour about midnight, and then went on again. I wished several times that I could see the ground. I'd like to have known if there were any fresh trails in it.

At dawn we must have been a good seventy-five miles north of Clinger's ranch. And suddenly, so close it scared hell out of me, I heard a volley of rapid shots.

The sounds came from directly ahead, on the other side of a rounded, brushy knoll. First thing I did was look around for someplace to hide. The only cover was a brush-choked gully a couple of hundred yards to our right. It was deep enough to hide us, but not deep enough to hide the horse. I reined toward it, kicking the horse in the ribs. He broke into a trot.

I rode him down into the gully where the brush was highest, and slid to the ground. I lifted Edith Clinger down, tied the horse, and said, "Stay here. Keep the horse as quiet as you can. I'll be back as soon as I see what's going on."

She started to say something but choked it back. I left her and worked my way along the gully in the direction from which the shots had come.

It was slow work, and it was hard not to make any noise. When I got almost to the top of the knoll, I looked back. I could see my horse's head when he raised it, but most of the time he kept it down. Apparently he had been able to find some grass.

I was crawling when I reached the top of the knoll. Even before I did, I knew what I was going to see. There was a little breeze blowing toward me out of the north, and it carried the strong, sweetish, sickly smell of death. I figured it had to come either from a buffalo hunters' camp or from an old stand, where dozens or maybe hundreds of buffalo carcasses had been left to rot.

I started to get up, thinking the shots must have come from the buffalo hunters' guns, then quickly dropped back again. Those reports had been sharp — the crack of ordinary rifles, not the deep boom of buffalo hunters' Sharps.

Even more cautiously than before, I continued crawling through the heavy brush. Finally I reached a place from which I could see the scene below.

It was a buffalo hunters' camp. On one side of it there was a wide, dry stream-bed. No water ran in the stream, but holes had been dug in the sand and they had filled with water.

There were three wagons, their tongues resting on the ground. A canvas shelter was stretched between four scrubby trees. Beyond, green hides were pegged out on the ground. Nearer, dry ones were stacked higher than a man.

These things I saw in a glance. But what caught and held my attention was the Indians. There must have been twenty of them at least. Some were riding around in a circle, yelling their fool heads off. Those that weren't were clustered around two white men lying on the ground.

I couldn't tell for sure, but it looked like both the white men were dead. The Indians were peeling the clothes off their bodies. Usually an Indian will at least take parts of the clothes belonging to a white man he's killed. These clothes must have been too stinking filthy even for an Indian. They threw them aside.

Some of them knelt beside the whitish, naked bodies, and I felt a little sick because I knew what they were doing to them. After they'd done their grisly work, one of them got a lance and plunged it down into the chest of one of the whites. He kept bearing down until the lance had gone clear through and buried itself in the ground.

Now the Indians left the two naked bodies

lying there and turned their attention to the wagons. They took coals from the hunters' fire and, holding them with sticks, threw them into the wagons. Smoke curled up, thickening as the fires grew.

I hoped Edith Clinger had sense enough to do what I'd told her. I glanced behind uneasily, half expecting to see her coming over the top of the knoll. If she came into sight now both of us were dead, and we'd be lucky if we died as quickly as those hunters had.

Suddenly, from down below, I heard a screech. It sounded a little like the scream of a panther that I'd heard once. I glanced at the bodies of the two white men and saw that one of them wasn't dead. He had been shot and mutilated, but apparently he'd only been unconscious while the Indians had been working on him. His breathing must have been so shallow that they hadn't noticed he was still alive.

But they noticed now. With howls of glee they returned to the man. One of them got a hot coal from the fire and, while four of the others held his arms and legs, laid it carefully on his naked belly.

The man screeched even louder than he had the first time. His first scream had been one of horror when he saw what they had done to him. This was different, a scream of pure agony.

I could feel the goose pimples breaking out on my arms and legs. The man screeched until he was out of breath and then his yells died to a series of bubbling groans.

Yelling, chattering, and laughing, the Indians now clustered around him. I'd always heard that you couldn't beat a Kiowa when it came to making a man die slow, and I guess what I'd heard was true. They kept that man screeching on and off for damn near half an hour, despite all that had already been done to him. And he never once lost consciousness.

The June sun down in north Texas isn't exactly cool. But it wasn't the heat that had so completely drenched my clothes with sweat. Even with my body sweating, though, I was cold. I was cold as ice, and shivering like I had a chill. I wanted desperately to put a bullet into that poor suffering hunter down there and end his misery, but I knew if I did I'd die the same way, and Edith Clinger would die in a way that was even worse.

All the time I watched, afraid to move, almost afraid to breathe for fear they'd discover me. I kept worrying about Edith Clinger and wondering if, after I'd been

26

gone so long, she'd stay put the way I'd told her to.

She might have heard the hunter's screams. She might even have heard the Indians' yells. But I didn't dare to move. Busy as those Indians were down there, it was possible one of them would spot me backing off. Indians don't miss much of what's going on around them, particularly when they know there are enemies around.

The hunter eventually died. Even from as far away as I was I could see the red splotches of blood on him. The Kiowas lost interest as soon as he died. They took his scalp and that of his friend. They mounted their horses and trotted them away, heading up the dry watercourse as if they had all the time in the world.

I waited until they were out of sight, then I moved. I eased back through the heavy brush.

It seemed to take forever for me to reach the place where I'd left Edith Clinger and my horse. I was still drenched with sweat. She took one look at my face, which I know must have been almost green, and her own face turned pale. I said quickly, "They're gone."

"What was it? What happened?"

"War party of Kiowas caught a couple of hunters off guard."

"A war party?"

"Painted up. Faces and upper bodies."

"What took you so long?"

I made a kind of sickly grin. "I was scared to move."

"And you had to watch?"

I tried to look like I didn't know what she meant. She said, "I heard the screams."

I said, "Let's get out of here."

"Aren't you going to bury them?"

"Hell no, I'm not. What good would it do anybody to bury 'em? They're dead."

"It just seemed like the decent thing to do." Her tone was faintly reproving.

I said harshly, "Ma'am, you wouldn't want to see the things that have been done to those men, and buryin' them wouldn't help anybody. I just want to get away from here and find a place where we can hide ourselves and this horse. When dark comes we'll travel again."

I mounted and lifted her up behind me. We rode out, staying in the heavy brush as much as possible. It wasn't likely that we'd run into another war party so close, but I took no chances. I kept my eyes moving all the time, scanning the slopes and ridge tops for signs of Indians.

Edith Clinger rode behind me, silent and subdued. I could tell she was wondering what would have happened to her if I hadn't come along. She knew now how impossible it would have been for her to walk through this country without getting caught.

As for myself, I was wondering if I really wanted to hunt buffalo down here below the Arkansas.

If I did, I sure wasn't going to get caught the way those two had back there. They had been taken so completely by surprise that they hadn't even fired a shot.

An hour after leaving the buffalo hunters' camp, I found a deep ravine, choked with mesquite and heavy brush. It was almost impenetrable, but it was just what I'd been looking for. I dismounted and lifted Edith Clinger down. I told her to follow the horse and to hold onto his tail. I led him down into the ravine, fighting my way through the choking brush.

At the bottom there was a damp spot in the sand. I scooped out a hole with my hands and let my horse drink all he would. I dug out another hole. When it was full, I filled both canteens.

Mrs. Clinger sat wearily in the shade with her back to a rock. I said, "You go to sleep. I'll watch. If anybody comes we'll hear 'em a long time before they see us."

She nodded, reassured. She gave me a

wan smile and closed her eyes.

Maybe she could sleep. But I knew I wasn't going to sleep today. The memory of those Kiowas working on the naked body of that hunter was too vivid in my mind.

Chapter 3

Along about sundown, Edith Clinger woke up. I figured she could use a little privacy, so I told her I'd be back before dark. I saddled my horse and led him up out of the ravine. I figured it would be a good idea if I knew where I was going. I wouldn't be able to see tracks at night and I wanted to avoid barging into Indians if I could.

I mounted as soon as I was out of the worst of the brush and rode cautiously north. I kept a sharp eye on the ridge tops as well as studying the ground. I crossed a river that was nearly dry, which I guessed was the Canadian. Pretty soon I struck a trail.

It wasn't an Indian trail. It was the trail of the wagons that had belonged to the buffalo hunters in that camp back there. It was pretty well rutted, almost a two-track road, as if the wagons had traveled it back and forth a good many times.

This told me that there was either a settlement not far away, or a larger camp. I swung around and returned to the ravine where Edith Clinger was. I made a lot of racket going down through the brush, figuring she'd know it was me. When I got to where we'd camped, she wasn't anywhere in sight. Pretty soon she came from behind a heavy clump of brush, the shotgun in her hands. I grinned at her. She looked scared, but not so scared she hadn't been able to make a try at defending herself. She'd thought I might be an Indian and, if I had been, I'd have got my pants full of buckshot before I knew what was going on. I looked at her approvingly and said, "There's a road north of here about a mile. I figure we'll follow it a ways. Likely there's either a settlement or a big buffalo hunters' camp at the end of it."

She nodded. She had everything ready, piled neatly on the ground and hidden behind a clump of brush. She brought it to me and I tied it on behind the saddle. I mounted and lifted her up and the horse fought his way up out of the brush-choked ravine.

The sun had dropped behind the horizon and stained the high clouds overhead a brilliant pink. I said, "Pretty, ain't it?"

"It's beautiful."

I asked, "Where'd you come from, ma'am?"

"Illinois. I was raised on a farm in eastern Illinois."

"Meet your husband there?"

"Yes. His brother had a farm near ours. I met him when he was visiting his brother. He told me about his ranch out here and asked me to marry him."

I didn't pursue it any further because I didn't want to pry. After a while she asked, "Are you a native of Texas, Mr. Burdett?"

"No, ma'am. I came out here after the war. My pa was a sharecropper in Georgia and I was glad enough to get away and join the army when the war broke out. I was in for four years, and when I went back home there was nothing there. Sherman's army had burned our house and all the other buildings. They'd used the fences for firewood and they'd dragged rails back and forth across the fields. My pa and ma were gone and nobody knew where. I hunted for most of a year but I never found a trace of them."

"How terrible."

"No, ma'am. It wasn't terrible. I was a grown man an' they knew that. Wherever they are, if they're still alive, I expect they're doin' better than they ever did on that wore-out little farm."

"And then you came west?"

"Yes, ma'am. Pretty near ten years ago. I got a job on a ranch down by Goliad. I made a couple of trips up the trail to Kansas with cattle. Once to Baxter Springs an' once to Wichita. I got laid off my job this last winter. If I hadn't got a job breaking horses, I'd probably have starved. I guess it was kind of the last straw, gettin' laid off for the winter like that. It told me something I hadn't thought of before. They'll use you up, an' when there's nothing left they'll throw you away. So I made up my mind that, one way or another, I was going to have a place of my own. And a family, maybe, if I can find a woman to say yes to me."

"I hope you do find one, Mr. Burdett. Then again, I am sure you will."

We crossed the river and struck the road I'd found while there was still gray enough in the sky to see it. I turned into it, hoping I wouldn't lose it in the dark. It wasn't likely, I discovered, because my horse stayed with it, breaking into an eager trot. He knew there was a settlement at the end of that road, and to him a settlement meant grain and other horses and some rest.

We traveled for three hours. I tried to make the horse walk but he kept breaking into a trot. I knew that gait was hard on Edith Clinger, but the damn horse just didn't want to walk. Finally, I gave up trying. Mrs. Clinger seemed to be getting along all right.

It must have been around ten or eleven o'clock when I saw some lights ahead. I stopped and studied them to make sure they were white men's lights and not the fires of an Indian camp. I decided they were white men's lights and started on again, and right then I saw the walls of an old fort off the road and north of it by a few hundred yards.

The moon was up by now and we could see them pretty plain. I'd heard of the place but I hadn't known there was a settlement nearby. I said, "They call it Adobe Walls, ma'am. It used to be a trading post. It was built by the Bents around thirty years ago, but I guess they found out that tradin' with Comanches an' Kiowas wasn't the same as tradin' with Cheyennes. They gave it up, just went off and left it. The Indians burned it. Those walls are all that's left."

About a hundred yards away from the settlement, I let out a yell, "Hey! I'm comin' in!" This way nobody would think we were Indians and start shooting at us. We rode into the settlement. I dismounted and lifted Mrs. Clinger down. Men came from the buildings and clustered around us, most of them holding guns. I said, "I'm Jess Burdett and this here's Mrs. Clinger from down south a ways." I didn't mention the way she looked. I didn't figure it was up to me to do her explaining for her. And I didn't want anybody getting the idea that I was running off with her. I'd have enough trouble without anybody thinking that.

I looked around. There were four buildings in all, hastily and roughly built. At one end there was a store built of pickets set upright in a trench. It was about sixty feet long and thirty feet wide and the walls didn't even keep out the wind. But they did hold up the roof, which was made of sod.

I found out later that it was a store belonging to Charlie Myers. He had formerly been a hide hunter himself, but had given it up and was now a hide buyer and a merchant on the side. He had come down here from Dodge City early in the spring and had helped found the settlement.

Adjoining Myers' store was a picket corral, two hundred by two hundred feet, and south of it was a sod saloon owned by a man named Hanrahan. It was twenty-five by sixty feet and it, too, had a sod roof supported by stout poles. Between these two buildings, and smaller than either, was a smithy owned by a blacksmith named O'Keefe. It was constructed of poles driven into the ground and was even more open to the weather than was Myers' store. The fourth building in the settlement was a sod house, south of Hanrahan's saloon, in which a man named Charles Rath had a store.

I was startled to hear a woman's voice. She came pushing toward us through the crowd, strong looking, wearing a dark skirt with an apron over it. I later learned that she and her husband, William Olds, ran a restaurant in the rear of Charles Rath's store.

She took charge of Edith Clinger immediately, clucking with outrage and sympathy when she saw the condition of Edith's face. Since she was the only woman at Adobe Walls, which was the name given the settlement despite the mile that separated it from Bent's old trading post, I suppose she was overjoyed to have another woman to keep her company.

I waited until the women had gone inside. Then I said, "Indians jumped a camp a ways west of here this morning. Killed two hunters and burned their camp."

A man whose face I couldn't see in the darkness said, "That sounds like Plummer's camp." He turned his head and shouted, "Plummer! Hey Joe!"

Plummer came out of Hanrahan's saloon, wiping his mouth with the back of his hand. The same voice shouted, "This stranger says Indians attacked your camp this morning an' killed Tom an' Dave!"

Plummer hurried to me, pushing roughly through the crowd. "Where was this at?" he asked.

I said, "West a ways on the bank of a dry creek. Happened about dawn this morning. Right after that, Mrs. Clinger and me holed up for the day in a brushy ravine. Soon's it got dark, we rode out."

A man said, "That's your camp, sure as hell, Joe. It's about three hours west of here. Only one anywheres near the place he says he was."

Plummer asked, "You bury 'em?"

I said, "Nope. It wouldn't have done any good."

Plummer grumbled, "Might have kep' the wolves from pickin' at 'em." He was staring at me as if I'd had something to do with it. He asked, "Did you go down there an' make sure they both was dead?"

"Nope."

"How come? One of 'em might still have been alive." There was anger now in Plummer's voice.

I said, "No chance of that. The Indians drove a stake down through the chest of one of 'em. They spent half an hour killin' the other one."

"And you just sat there an' watched?"

I was beginning to get a little mad myself.

I said, "Just what the hell would you have done, mister big mouth? There were twenty Indians in that party, all painted up for trouble an' there was only one of me."

"I'd have put the one they was workin' on out of his misery. That's what I'd have done."

I said, "You're a liar. You'd have done the same thing I did." I was ready to fight by now and I hoped he'd take me up on calling him a liar in front of everyone. He didn't, though. He called out, "Who'll go with me?"

Half a dozen men agreed to go and the group scattered, those with Plummer going to the corral, the others heading back toward Hanrahan's saloon. Someone offered me a drink and another man said, "Don't pay no mind to Plummer, Mr. Burdett. Both Tom Wallace an' Dave Dudley was good friends of his, besides workin' for him. Nobody would have done any more'n you did. Hell, them Indians could've been watching that camp for a couple of hours to see if anybody else would show up."

I went into the saloon. It had a packed earth floor that was slick and muddy on top, probably from things being spilled on it. There was a long bar made out of poles that had been hewn flat on one side. The whiskey was in kegs behind it.

As soon as we could see each other in the light from the lanterns hanging from the ceiling poles, the man with me stuck out his hand and said he was Karl Lutz. He ordered a drink for me and paid for it. After that I bought him one. I was finishing it when I heard Plummer and those with him gallop away, heading west toward his camp.

Hanrahan was behind the bar serving drinks. He came over and introduced himself. I could see that he was curious about how Edith got all beat up, but he was too polite to ask. I figured I'd just as well get everybody's curiosity satisfied before they started making wild guesses, so I said, "I found Mrs. Clinger about seventy-five miles south of here. Her husband had beat her up and she was leaving, heading north on foot. I couldn't just leave her, walking, a hundred and fifty miles from anywhere, so I put her up behind me and brought her here."

"How long ago was that?"

"Two days."

"What you going to do when her husband catches up with you?" Hanrahan was grinning at me.

I said, "I got no interest in the woman other than just to get her someplace safe. Well, I done that. But if her husband pushes me, by God I might have to give him a little of what he gave her."

Hanrahan asked, "Where you headin' for, if that ain't too touchy a thing to ask?"

I said, "I was heading north to get me a job hunting buffalo."

Down the bar a ways a man called, "You got one, Mr. Burdett." He pushed past the men between us and stuck out his hand. "I'm Charlie Myers. You can work for me. You want to hunt or skin?"

I said, "Hunt."

"Got any experience?"

"Not hunting buffalo. I've worked cattle and been on two drives up out of Texas to the rails. I was four years in the war."

"Winning or losing side?"

"Losing." I'd never been touchy about the war the way some men still were. It was over and done with a long time ago.

Myers said, "All right. I'll give you a try. I'll put you out with one of my experienced hunters and let him show you how."

Someone asked, "Who you goin' to put him with, Charlie?"

"Hagerman."

A couple of men laughed. "If he can't learn from Hagerman, then he can't learn."

Karl Lutz, the man who had bought me the drink, now ordered another one. I asked,

"What did he mean by that?"

Lutz said, "Hagerman's kinda touched in the head. Comanches killed his wife down south of here last fall. He tried trackin' 'em but lost the trail. Now he figures that as long as he can't find the ones that did it, he'll get even with the whole damn tribe. Killin' their buffalo is the quickest way. He's the best that Myers has got. Kills twice as many buffalo as anybody else. He figures that when they're gone, the redskins will have to starve."

I said, "They will, too."

Lutz said, "Somebody's goin' to kill the buffalo, whether we do or not. White men keep movin' west. Cattle need the grass."

It was the same reasoning I'd used to justify myself. And certainly, after what I'd seen this morning, I should have no reason to sympathize with the Indians.

But I knew they'd been pushed into what they'd done. I couldn't blame them for hating the men who killed their buffalo and used only the hides, leaving the rest to rot.

Chapter 4

It was late by this time, close to midnight. Some of the men began drifting away from the saloon, those who regularly slept outside. Those who slept inside the saloon began putting their blankets down and turning in, oblivious of the noise that still continued inside the place. I wasn't particularly tired, but I could see that Hanrahan was closing up. I told Karl Lutz good night and went outside. I led my horse out away from the building until I could feel long grass rustling beneath my feet. I unsaddled and picketed him, then carried my saddle and bridle back. I made my bed against the wall of Myers' store. I could see the place I had picketed my horse. Beyond his dimly seen shape was visible the main horse herd, grazing loose. I wondered why the Indians hadn't run them off. Maybe there hadn't been any Indians in the vicinity until recently.

I went to sleep even before all the noise inside the settlement had ceased. I woke up once to hear snores nearby, to hear the half dozen or so horses moving around in the corral, to hear a wolf howl far out in the hills. I did not awake again until the sky was light.

I got up. I walked to the stream and washed. I shaved, then put my things back in the saddlebags. The sun was coming up as I headed for Rath's store and the restaurant Olds and his wife ran at the rear of it.

This hide hunters camp near Adobe Walls was no place for the squeamish, I decided as I walked. Hanging over everything was the cloying smell of death, coming from the piled-up dry buffalo hides awaiting shipment to Dodge City, and from the clothes and wagons of the hunters and skinners themselves. There were no laundresses here, so clothing seldom got washed. Water was scarce in the hunters' camps, so they almost never bathed. I suppose a man could get used to the smell, just as he did to most everything else. Perhaps even to the point where he wouldn't notice it until a fresh breeze that had been blowing into his face from the prairie stopped suddenly.

But the stink of decaying flesh was not the only smell. There was the smell of the corral, of horses, of cooking and of smoke, both wood and tobacco, and of the men themselves, to say nothing of the smell of li-

44

quor, which was consumed here in great quantities.

The smells were not all unpleasant ones. There was the smell of the hot prairie, too, and of a wind that scoured clean a thousand miles of empty prairie land. There was the smell of sage, pungent and pleasant and even, sometimes, a fleeting odor of cedar and pinon pine, caught so briefly it almost seemed I had imagined it.

The buildings were ugly, hastily constructed, and temporary. When this hunting season was done, or when the buffalo ceased to be plentiful, it would be abandoned and promptly destroyed by the Indians, to whom it was an ugly scar on an otherwise beautiful land.

Across the back of Rath's store there was a long counter or bar similar to the one in Hanrahan's saloon, except that it was lower. In front of it were crudely built benches. Half a dozen men were already sitting there, waiting to be served. Several of them nodded shortly to me as I sat down. All were bearded, and all wore hats.

Behind the counter, Olds, his wife, and Edith Clinger were working hard. There was a big cast-iron stove they had freighted here from Dodge. Meat was frying in huge pans on it. Potatoes were sizzling in a couple of other pans. The meat was, I knew, buffalo hump and tongue. The potatoes were frying in buffalo grease.

Olds brought all of us tin cups and plates, and gave each of us a knife and fork. He brought a huge pot of coffee and filled the cups. Mrs. Olds glanced around at me once, then turned away again. Edith Clinger avoided my glance.

As soon as the meat was cooked, Olds set platters out. By this time other men had drifted in. I helped myself to as much as I figured I could eat and passed both platters on. Some of the others finished before I did. Each left half a dollar on the counter beside his empty plate.

I paid for my meal and went outside. Five troopers and a bearded civilian were standing about fifty yards away, talking among themselves. I hadn't seen them the night before, but that didn't mean they had not been here. Karl Lutz came up beside me and I asked, "What are they doing here?"

He shrugged. "Nobody seems to know. One of them troopers said they was huntin' horse thieves, but why the hell would the Army be huntin' horse thieves away out here?"

"Who's the civilian? He looks like he might be half Indian."

"He is. Amos Chapman is his name. He

come with them troopers from Fort Supply, over in Indian territory."

"What do *you* think they're doin' here?"

"Well hell, everybody knows huntin' buffalo below the Arkansas is agin' the law. The gov'mint made a treaty with the Indians about seven years ago, the Medicine Lodge Treaty. I figure them troopers is here findin' out just who's huntin' buffalo. I figure they'll go back an' pretty soon a whole goddamn troop will show up here an' start makin' arrests."

"The Army can't arrest civilians."

"They can if they bring a U.S. Marshal along with them."

"How long have they been here?"

"Since night before last. I figure they'll pull out today."

Two of the troopers left the group. They headed out into the grassy meadow, on the opposite side of the settlement from the horse herd, to where their horses were picketed. Chapman and the other three walked farther out away from the buildings, still talking among themselves. Pretty soon Hanrahan and Charlie Myers came from the saloon and crossed to where they were.

Chapman, Hanrahan, and Myers began to talk. I wanted to ask Myers when I could start hunting buffalo, so I headed toward them. The soldiers had drifted off a ways and were carrying on their own conversation. Myers, Hanrahan, and Chapman all had their backs to me.

I guess they didn't hear me until I was a few feet away. I must have startled them because they stopped talking suddenly and whirled around. Their faces looked like the faces of kids caught with their hands in the jam jar, and I wondered what the hell they could have been talking about to make them look at me like that. Something they sure didn't want me to hear. Something they didn't want anyone to hear.

I said, "Sorry to interrupt. I just wanted to ask when I'm supposed to go out to Hagerman's camp."

Myers was irritated and it showed. He said shortly, "I'll let you know."

I was a little irritated myself. I didn't know what they were hiding and I didn't care. But I didn't like getting snapped at when I hadn't done anything I shouldn't have. I said angrily, "You do that. You just do that," and I turned and walked away.

Myers called, "Mr. Burdett!"

I stopped and turned my head. Myers grinned at me. "Sorry," he said.

Well, he was a big, likeable man with an easygoing manner about him and his grin was catching. I grinned back and said, "Forget it." I went back to the buildings and the three resumed their conversation. Myers wasn't angry at me, so the reason for his edginess had to be in whatever they were talking about.

I walked out into the meadow and led my horse to water, then picketed him again where the grass was good. By the time I got through, the troopers who had gone after their horses had returned. The four and Amos Chapman mounted, nodded at Myers and Hanrahan and rode away, heading toward the northeast.

Myers and Hanrahan stayed out in the meadow. After a few minutes, Rath and two other men walked to where they were. Later I found out that the two other men were John and Wright Mooars, who were in the freighting business. They owned a lot of the big hide wagons drawn up in a line beside Myers' corral, and they were the ones who had originally pushed the idea of establishing a post here at Adobe Walls.

The five men watched Chapman and the troopers until they had disappeared. I could tell they were talking, even though they had their backs to the buildings.

It was possible, of course, that Chapman had only come to order them to abandon

Adobe Walls and stop hunting below the Arkansas. But if that was it, why all the secrecy? Why Myers' edginess with me? Every hunter here knew he was breaking the law by hunting below the Arkansas. There would be no reason to keep a desist order from the Army a secret. No reason at all.

I killed a couple of hours by walking around and looking at the stacks of dry buffalo hides and examining the big, ponderous hide wagons. I bought a new Sharps fifty-caliber buffalo gun at Myers' store and five hundred rimfire cartridges for it. I also bought a tripod on which to rest the barrel. I left these things at the store for safekeeping and went outside again.

I met Edith Clinger coming out of Rath's. She would have gone on by with only a short nod, but I stepped squarely in front of her, making it impossible.

Her face looked much better today than it had yesterday. I suppose Mrs. Olds had put buffalo meat on the bruises to draw some of the swelling and discoloration out. Edith's eyes looked more normal. Her mouth was no longer swelled, though she still had scabs on her lips. I suddenly realized that she was a damn pretty woman. She'd be prettier if she smiled, but I suppose it hurt considerably to smile.

I said, "Well, you look fine today."

"Thank you, Mr. Burdett."

I said, "I don't let everybody do this, but you can call me Jess."

It wasn't very funny, but it brought a faint smile to her mouth. I said, "It looks like you've got yourself a job."

"Yes. Mrs. Olds asked if I would help."

"And you're through now until noon?"

"That's right."

"You must have gotten up pretty early."

"I'm used to getting up early, Mr. Burdett."

"Jess."

"Jess." There was the smile again.

Her forehead clouded with thought, and I caught myself adding up the days and trying to figure when her husband would arrive. We'd lain around all day yesterday, and we hadn't traveled too hard before that because I hadn't wanted to push my horse, carrying double, any more than I had to.

She'd said her husband would be gone several days. I supposed that meant two or three. She turned her head now and looked toward the south and I asked, "How long was he going to be away? You said several days, but you didn't say how many."

"Two days. Or three. He is not well-liked at Butterworth's, so I doubt if he would stay

51

any longer than necessary."

I said, "We lost a day yesterday, lyin' around in that ravine. I figure all we can count on is today. If he pushes his horse, he could get here tomorrow, and I reckon that he will."

"He may not come at all."

I looked at her face. She was slightly flushed. I said, "He'll come, all right. Man that's got as pretty a woman as you ain't likely to let her get away."

The color of her face deepened to an uncomfortable pink. She said, without looking straight at me, "That will not be your concern, Mr. Burdett. I will handle my husband when he comes. There is no need for him even to know that you brought me here."

I said, "No need? These buffalo hunters here are as gossipy as a bunch of old women. Your husband will know about me five minutes after he rides in."

"Well, there is still no reason for you to mix into it. What has happened is between my husband and myself."

I said, "I just hope you can keep it that way, Mrs. Clinger. I hope you can."

She stepped aside and went on past. She said, "Good day, Mr. Burdett."

She was angry with me now. I didn't know why because I hadn't said anything out of the way. I'd said she was pretty, but that was the truth and she probably knew it anyway.

Maybe she was angry because I'd brought up the subject of her husband. Or maybe she wasn't angry at all, only frightened and worried about what was going to happen when her husband did arrive.

I felt an odd and unexpected uneasiness, almost as if a cloud had passed across the sun. I glanced up at the sky. It was flawless blue, without a cloud in sight. Shrugging, I went into Hanrahan's, crossed to the bar, and ordered myself a drink. Myers would let me know when it was time to go out to Hagerman's hunting camp. Until then, I might just as well take it easy and try to stop worrying.

Chapter 5

About mid-morning Joe Plummer came riding in along with the half dozen men who had volunteered to go to his camp with him last night. They had two extra horses that Plummer was leading. On each was the body of a man wrapped in a blanket and lashed down with rope. Plummer scowled at me as he swung to the ground and tied his horse to the rail in front of the saloon. He went inside immediately, without even looking at the men with him. He must need a drink, but then anyone would after seeing the things that had been done to his friends. The men with Plummer tied their horses and followed him into the saloon.

Myers came out of his store and saw the horses tied to the saloon rail. He walked over to me and said, "Somebody's got to dig graves for them two. You ain't doing anything. Want the job?"

I shrugged. I'd come to hunt buffalo, but I'd spent most of my money earlier buying the new Sharps fifty caliber and cartridges for it. Myers said, "Five dollars a grave."

54

I nodded. He said, "Get a shovel in the shed behind my store. Anywhere out there in the meadow ought to do. Diggin' ought to be easy there."

I went to the shed and got a shovel and grubbing hoe. I carried them about fifty yards away from the buildings. I marked out both graves first and then began to dig.

I didn't hurry, but I kept at it. The sun climbed up the sky and started down toward the horizon in the west. I made the graves seven feet long, two wide, and six feet deep. I didn't want Myers saying I hadn't earned what he was paying me.

It was mid-afternoon by the time I finished and climbed out. Looking toward the saloon I saw that the two horses with the bodies on them were gone. The bodies were in the back of a wagon. They had been wrapped with canvas. There weren't any coffins at Adobe Walls and no sawed lumber to make them with.

Seeing I had finished, Myers came out in front of his store. He fired a shotgun into the air. Everybody came hurrying toward him. Myers yelled, "We're buryin' Wallace an' Dudley. Come on, everyone!"

A group formed around the wagon in which the two bodies lay. Olds and his wife were there and so was Edith Clinger. Most of the men had guns, either revolvers in belt holsters or rifles. Edith Clinger carried her old double-barreled shotgun. A team was hitched to the wagon. Myers climbed to the seat and started toward the graves.

I looked for Plummer and finally spotted him in the crowd. His eyes were bloodshot and his mouth was slack. I guessed he had been drinking ever since getting back, but he wasn't drunk. He walked without staggering.

I let the little procession pass me and then fell in behind. I knew I'd be expected to fill the graves in afterward, and besides, I figured everybody in this small a community ought to attend out of respect.

The wagon was backed up to the graves and the bodies lifted down. Myers supervised the laying of ropes on the ground, and the bodies were laid one after the other on the ropes. Myers picked men to man the ropes, then took a small dog-eared Bible out of his pocket and opened it. He waited until everyone had quieted. He then began to read.

Edith Clinger stood with her head bowed, the shotgun resting on the ground in front of her. Once she glanced up, her gaze going toward the south, then sweeping west to the direction from which we had approached the settlement. My glance followed hers but I saw nothing. Only the crumbling, adobe walls of Bent's old trading post.

Myers began to read. I wondered how many times he had done this in the past. There was no hesitation in him and no uncertainty. He seemed to know which passages he ought to read and where to find them in the book.

When he had finished he raised his head and nodded to the men holding the ropes. One by one they lifted the bodies with the ropes, positioned them over the graves, and lowered them. Afterward they pulled out the ropes and coiled them up. Myers stepped to the graves and sprinkled a handful of earth into each one of them. He climbed to the wagon seat and drove back toward the corral. The others followed. I remained behind. When everyone had gone, I filled in the graves, mounding the excess dirt neatly over them.

It was hot and I was sweating heavily. I glanced south and west again, wondering about Clinger, wondering when he was going to come. I wasn't afraid of him, but I sure wasn't looking forward to his arrival. I figured he'd force a fight with me and I had no idea whether it would be with guns or fists. What I did know was that I didn't want to kill the man. If I did, everybody would say I had done it because I wanted his wife, and that wasn't true. I'd kill him to keep from getting killed myself, and I'd probably kill him if it was necessary to keep him from beating her up again, but I'd avoid it if I could.

Leaning on the shovel, I stared at the little settlement. Its founders had certainly known what they were doing when they located it. It sat on the bank of a small stream and would ordinarily have plenty of water available. However, knowing that many streams dry up in late summer, they had dug a well inside the corral and had installed a pump in it.

Grassy meadowland surrounded the settlement and there was a clear view in all directions. Indians would never have cover within rifle range of the buildings. Furthermore, the meadow provided plenty of grass for the horse herd and kept them near the buildings without anybody herding them.

I walked back and returned the shovel and grubbing hoe to the shed. I hadn't eaten any dinner and I was hungry. I went into Rath's store and back to the restaurant at the rear. Mrs. Olds was working at the stove. I sat down and said, "I was busy digging those graves and didn't get in for dinner. Got anything a man can eat?"

She looked at me. "Stew's hot. Want some of that?"

"Yes, ma'am."

She dished up some stew made of buffalo meat and potatoes and carrots and poured me a tin cup of coffee. She cut me a chunk of bread to go with it. Pretty soon she said, "That husband of hers is goin' to come after her."

I said, "Yes, ma'am. I reckon so."

"She ain't no match for him. She ain't going to be able to use that shotgun when the time comes, no matter what she thinks."

I said, "No, ma'am. I don't figure she can."

She was silent a moment and finally she said, "Unless somebody stops him, he's goin' to take her back with him. And beat her again the way he did before."

I wanted to tell her it wasn't any business of mine, or hers, either, for that matter. But I didn't. Instead I said, "Somebody will stop him, ma'am."

"Not my Bill. He says anybody that butts in between a husband an' wife deserves exactly what he gets."

"He's likely right."

"Then you won't help that girl?"

"I didn't say that. I just ain't going to

make any promises to you."

It wasn't much of a commitment, but it seemed to satisfy her. Smiling faintly she brought me a big piece of dried apple pie and refilled my coffee cup.

I put half a dollar on the counter and got up and left. I went into Myers' store and bought three cigars. He paid me the ten dollars for digging the graves, taking out what I owed for the cigars. I went out, biting off the end of one. Standing in front of the store, I lighted it.

I was tired, but it was a muscular tiredness that feels kind of pleasant when the hard work is over with. I sat down on a bench, enjoying my cigar.

Glancing north, I saw a horseman approaching the settlement. He had just come over a low ridge and was riding at a steady trot.

I couldn't help stiffening. I hitched my gun holster around just a little bit, so I could get the gun out easily. Maybe it wasn't Clinger. He shouldn't be coming from the north. But it was possible he'd missed this settlement, had gone by, had then struck the road leading to Dodge City, and had come back.

Edith hadn't described her husband to me, so I didn't know if this was the man or not. He was tall, I'd have said around six feet. He was thin, but you could tell he was powerful. He wore gray homespun pants and a blue Army shirt that was faded on the chest, back, and under the arms from sweat. He had a wide-brimmed, shapeless hat, pulled well down in front to shade his eyes. You couldn't say he had either a beard or mustache, but he hadn't shaved for a couple of weeks at least. His eyes were gray and looked right through a man. He stopped in front of me and I exhaled a mouthful of smoke. He said, "Howdy."

I nodded. He studied me a few minutes and finally he said, "I'm Sam Argo. I'm lookin' for a man named Curt DeValois." He pronounced it Devaloy.

Myers came out of the store behind me. I thought there wasn't much going on around here that Myers missed. He said, "I'm Charlie Myers. What's this man look like?"

"Short. Made like a bull. Yeller hair an' blue eyes."

I was watching Myers' face. Maybe he hid it from Argo, but he didn't hide it from me. He knew this DeValois, though maybe not by that name. He asked, "What's he wanted for?"

"Killed a farm girl up near Dodge. Forced her, an' when she fought, he just plain beat the girl to death."

"You a lawman, are you?"

"You might say that. I figure to see he goes back to Dodge for trial."

"Got a badge or anything?"

"I got this." Argo pulled a wanted poster out of his pocket. It was folded and dog-eared. He tossed it down to Myers, who caught it and unfolded it. At the top it said, "$500 reward."

Myers said, "You're a bounty hunter then."

"Somethin' wrong with that?"

"I didn't say anything was wrong with it."

Karl Lutz had come from the saloon. He stood there listening but not saying anything. Myers handed the wanted poster to him and he read it carefully. He handed it back, still without saying anything. Myers folded it and handed it up to Argo, who was still on his horse. Unexpectedly, Lutz said, "Dirty goddamn bounty hunter! You'd turn your own brother in for fifty bucks."

The hunter looked straight at him. His eyes had narrowed a little and his mouth was a firmer, straighter line. He said, "If he'd done what DeValois did to that girl, you're damned right I would." He turned his attention back to Myers. "Is he here?"

Myers said, "Well, I don't like bounty

hunters much, but I like woman killers less. The description fits Cass Gregory. He's at Forney's camp, fifteen miles southeast of here. You go south until you hit the Canadian. You follow it about ten miles until you come to a crik runnin' into it from the south. Follow that an' you'll hit Forney's camp."

Argo nodded. "Thanks, Mr. Myers."

"Watch out fer Indians. They killed two skinners west of here a couple of days ago."

"I'll watch." Argo looked long and hard at Lutz, then turned his horse and rode away.

Lutz waited until he was out of sight. Then he headed for the corral. He got his horse and rode out, going the same way Argo had.

Myers, who had come out of the store, walked to the corner of the building and stared after him. I asked, "Lutz a friend of this Gregory?"

Myers shrugged. "They know each other."

"Maybe he figures to cut in on the reward."

Myers shrugged again. "Or warn Gregory so he can get away."

"You think Gregory's the one?"

"Hell, I don't know. He's a good skinner. Forney likes his work."

He stood there for a few minutes. Finally

he asked, "You goin' to take on this Clinger when he comes?"

I said, "A man's a fool that gets between a husband and his wife." I was quoting Olds.

"You're already in between. You might not have any choice."

The cigar was getting shorter. I asked, "When do you want me to go out to Hagerman's camp?"

"I'm goin' down there day after tomorrow for a load of hides. That soon enough?"

"That's soon enough." I realized with some surprise that I wasn't in any hurry to go to Hagerman's hunting camp. The reason was that I wanted to be here when Edith Clinger's husband came.

I guessed I was the damn fool Olds had been talking about. But I was already between Edith Clinger and her husband. Bringing her here had put me there.

Chapter 6

Argo came back late that night, cursing and grumbling to himself. Cass Gregory was gone, he said, and nobody would say where he was. He wanted to know if anybody had seen Lutz, but nobody had. Argo went into Hanrahan's saloon, leaving his horse tied out in front.

I turned in around ten, once more making my bed along the wall of Myers' store. I had not turned my horse in with the others because I knew Indians were in the vicinity. I figured it was just a matter of time until they got bold enough to run the horse herd off. I didn't want to lose my horse when they did.

The following morning Clinger still had not shown up. I wondered if Indians had gotten him, or if he had decided not to come.

I had breakfast at the counter in the rear of Rath's store. The menu was the same as it had been yesterday. I supposed it didn't change much, buffalo meat being all that was available. Edith Clinger was quiet, frightened I supposed.

Outside afterward, I sat down on the bench and lighted a cigar. A wagon was approaching from the south and I watched it curiously.

It halted directly in front of Hanrahan's saloon. Two men sat up on the wagon seat. Both were dirty and bearded. One of them stood up and bawled in a heavily Irish voice, "Hey now, boys, come see what O'Malley's got! Lookin's free, but if ye want more than that, it'll cost ye five."

He climbed down from the wagon seat as men began gathering curiously. When a dozen or so were present, he went to the rear of the wagon and flung aside the canvas flap.

Now I'm as curious as the next man, so I walked over to where I could see.

At first I couldn't see anything because the inside of the wagon was so dark. Then I saw a dim figure crouched against the side. It was an Indian girl, naked as the day she was born. There was a heavy rope tied around her neck and her hands were tied in back of her. O'Malley looked toward the saloon and bawled again, "Come on out here, boys, an' see what O'Malley's got. By God, I'll be makin' more money in a week with her than I'd be makin' in a season huntin' buffalo!"

More men came from the saloon and

joined the crowd at the rear of the wagon. O'Malley let them look, then closed the flap again. He climbed to the wagon seat, chucking delightedly. "We'll be over by the crik, boys. Git your money an' come along!"

His partner clucked to the team and the wagon rumbled away, headed toward the creek. He stopped about a hundred yards away. The two men got down and unhitched their team. They took the harness off and turned the horses loose. The animals trotted off a ways, rolled, then got up and headed toward the horse herd a quarter mile away.

I looked around and saw Edith and Mrs. Olds standing in front of Rath's store. Mrs. Olds was red-faced and furious. She turned and went back inside. A few moments later I could hear her voice, shrill and outraged. Myers stood in the doorway of his store. He hadn't looked inside the wagon. He asked now, "What have they got, a squaw?"

I said, "Uh huh. Young one. Naked as a jaybird with a rope around her neck."

Myers was scowling, but he didn't say anything. I asked, "You going to let them keep her here?"

He looked at me. "Let them? Hell, I ain't got nothing to say about what they do. I don't own this place. All I own is this here store."

I said, "The Comanches will miss her and follow the trail here."

"You think I don't know that?"

Already men were streaming toward the wagon. Before the two horses had reached the horse herd, four men already stood in line. O'Malley roared, "All right, boys, come on. First ones is goin' to have it best!"

Olds came out of Rath's store, his greasy apron still tied around his waist. He came over to Myers and said, "We got to stop it. I don't know how, but we got to try."

Myers asked, "Your wife?"

"Her an' that other woman. They're both as mad as a teased rattler."

The line at O'Malley's wagon was now about twelve men long. Myers said sourly, "Tell her to go tell those men."

Olds grinned faintly. "You think she won't?"

Myers said, "Tell her. If a man tries it he's liable to get killed. It's been months since them men had a woman, an it'll be longer before they have another one. I ain't goin' to be the one to tell 'em that they can't."

Neither Olds nor Myers was thinking of the Indian girl. I doubted if Mrs. Olds was thinking of her either, as an individual at least. To everyone here, Indians were just animals. Mrs. Olds was incensed because

68

she considered what was going on an affront to all womanhood.

Olds shrugged and went back toward Rath's store. Halfway there he turned and looked around. I could tell he hated facing his wife again. He went into the store. Shortly afterward I heard Mrs. Olds shrilling at him. There now were almost twenty men in the line.

I felt sorry for the girl. She was going to be hurt and she might die before it was over with, but I knew as well as Myers did that any man who interfered would get killed for his pains. And besides, even if somebody did rescue her, what would they do with her? It was a cinch that O'Malley and his partner hadn't let her alone since capturing her. If she was to be turned loose, she'd make it back to her tribe and tell them what had happened and then all hell would break loose. Nor could she stay here. She was wild and as dangerous as any Indian brave, and she hated whites the way most of these whites hated Indians.

Mrs. Olds came storming out of Rath's store. She had a cleaver in her hand. She marched across toward the wagon, with Olds looking helplessly after her.

O'Malley saw her coming. The men in the line stared at her apprehensively, but they did not give up their places in the line.

Suddenly she charged toward them like a maddened buffalo. They scattered, having a healthy respect for the cleaver in her hand. She picked one man and went after him. Behind her, the line formed raggedly again.

Turning, she charged again. Once more the line of men scattered, each man content to stay just out of her reach. She picked a single individual and pursued him and again the line formed in back of her.

I glanced at Olds. His face was getting red. He started toward the wagon but Myers caught his arm. He said, "Let it alone, Bill. She got herself into this. Let her get herself out of it."

A man came climbing out of the wagon. He was busily buttoning up his pants. He saw Mrs. Olds and turned his back in embarrassment and finished buttoning. She charged toward him and somebody yelled, "Hey, Frank! Look out!"

Frank turned his head and saw her coming, less than ten feet away. He started to run, his pants still only partly fastened, Mrs. Olds about ten feet behind. Frank headed for Hanrahan's, but halfway there his pants, which were loose and baggy anyway, came down around his knees. They tripped him and he sprawled helplessly face downward on the ground.

I was grinning now. I couldn't help myself. I looked sideways at Olds and saw that he was grinning too. Myers choked, "Bill, if she sees you laughing, you're in more trouble than Frank."

Olds raised a hand to cover up his mouth. Frank was crawling now, on hands and knees. He hadn't taken time to try and get his pants up again. Mrs. Olds had stopped. She didn't seem to know what to do. She stared helplessly at his red-flannel-clad rump retreating so awkwardly before her.

Back at O'Malley's wagon, the men waiting in line were laughing uproariously. Mrs. Olds glanced back at them. Her own face turned a painful red.

Olds walked across to her. He didn't say anything. He just stood beside her. Seeing he was not pursued, Frank got up, pulled up his pants, and ran for the saloon. He disappeared inside.

Suddenly Mrs. Olds began to cry. She scurried toward the door of Rath's store and disappeared inside.

Olds turned his head and glared at the men waiting in line at the rear of O'Malley's wagon. He asked challengingly, "What the hell are you laughing at?"

The laughter stopped. Olds stared angrily

71

at them for a moment more. Then he turned and followed his wife into Rath's store.

Three men who had apparently changed their minds now left the line and hurried across to Hanrahan's. I saw that Myers wasn't grinning now. Nothing about the incident seemed funny any more.

Rath came out of his store. He said, "Come on, Charlie, let's talk to O'Malley."

"Why?" Myers asked.

"Maybe we can talk him into taking her someplace else."

The two walked across toward O'Malley's wagon. O'Malley saw them coming and he and Westerhoff met them halfway. Rath said, "How about taking your wagon over in the timber out of sight?"

"Why? Why the hell should I?"

"What you're doing is against the law. I can get a marshal down here from Dodge."

Westerhoff said, "What the hell are you talkin' about? That Injun gal is my wife. What a man does with his wife is his own damn business, ain't it?"

Rath looked at Myers helplessly. Westerhoff said, "You take the boys' fun away from 'em now, an' it ain't goin' to set too well. They might quit your goddamn hide camp. They might freight their hides to Dodge themselves. Then what the hell would you do with all the stuff you freighted here?"

Men had come from the saloon. They clustered around O'Malley, Westerhoff, Myers, and Rath. Rath's talk of getting a marshal here from Dodge had been pure bluff, and both O'Malley and Westerhoff had known it was. Neither Myers nor Rath wanted a U.S. Marshal here. This whole place was illegal and they knew it.

Myers and Rath gave up. Turning, they walked away from the group. Triumphantly, O'Malley began to make his sales pitch to the new arrivals. Some of them walked over and took places at the end of the line.

I felt someone watching me. I turned my head and saw Edith Clinger standing in the doorway of Rath's store. She came toward me and I met her halfway between the two stores. Her face was pale, making the bruises that still remained show up more plainly than before. She said, "Please. Can't you do anything?"

I asked, "What should I do? It's not my business."

"Make it your business. That poor girl in there. . . ."

I said, "That poor girl is a Comanche. She'd kill you as soon as look at you. Give her a chance and she'll crouch by a white man and work on him with her knife along with the best of them."

"But what they're doing. . . ."

I said, "So it isn't right. If I try to stop it, I'll have to fight every damn man in this settlement. I'd probably get myself killed for my pains."

Right then I wasn't feeling proud of myself. What was happening to the Indian girl ought to be stopped.

But hatred for Indians was as much a part of these men as the stink that clung to their clothes. Nobody was going to change it. Nobody could succeed in helping that Indian girl, and I'd never been one to try things that I knew could not be done.

I don't know whether the discussion would have continued or not. Right then I heard a shout.

Looking toward the sound, I saw a man riding toward the settlement from the south, trailing two horses, a body lashed face downward on the back of each.

The line at O'Malley's wagon broke up at once. Men poured from the stores and the saloon. Myers came out. "It's Anderson Moore," he said. "Them dead ones must be his skinners, Blue Billy and Antelope Jack." He hurried toward the three horses, which now were less than a hundred yards away.

Even from this distance I could see that

neither Blue Billy nor Antelope Jack had any hair. Their heads, where their scalps had been, were now masses of dried and blackened blood.

White-faced, Edith Clinger hurried back to Rath's and disappeared inside. I was thinking that the Indian girl would be lucky if someone didn't stick a knife in her. After this, she'd be lucky just to stay alive.

It didn't look as if O'Malley was going to get rich off the Indian girl the way he had planned. There wasn't going to be time. An Indian attack was shaping up. I was almost certain now that Amos Chapman had come here from Fort Supply to warn Myers and his partners about just such an attack.

When it would happen was anybody's guess. But I didn't figure the Comanches and Kiowas were going to wait until all the buffalo were gone before they tried to get rid of the buffalo hunters.

Chapter 7

Anderson Moore rode up in front of Myers' store, got down and tied his horse. Others took the halter ropes of the two led horses and tied them beside Moore's. The bodies of Blue Billy and Antelope Jack were still clothed. The Indians must have been interrupted before they could strip or mutilate them beyond the taking of their scalps.

Scalping a man loosens the flesh of the face and it sags downward, changing his appearance so as to make him almost unrecognizable even to those who know him best. I helped lift one of the dead men down and carry him inside. Then I went back out. Moore was just going into the saloon. Half a dozen men were following him, asking questions about what had happened out at his camp. I noticed that both O'Malley and Westerhoff now had rifles in their hands, probably in case any of Antelope Jack's or Blue Billy's friends got the notion of avenging them by killing the Indian girl. There was no longer a line behind O'Malley's wagon. What O'Malley had thought would be a profitable enterprise had turned sour. If trouble with the Indians continued, they'd probably be kept busy just defending her.

Myers came out. His face was grim. He said, "We need a couple more graves. You don't have to do it unless you want to, though."

I said, "I'll do it." I felt edgy and irritable and I knew some hard physical work would help. I got the shovel and went out to where the other two graves were. I marked out two more and went to work.

Occasionally I stopped to rest. When I did, I scanned the edges of the meadow and the surrounding slopes for Indians.

I finished the two graves a little after noon. I washed up and headed for Rath's to get my dinner.

Myers was at the counter, along with a couple of other men, just finishing up. Myers looked at me and asked, "Finished?"

I nodded. He fished a gold Eagle out of his pocket and gave it to me. I ordered my dinner. Edith Clinger was working at the stove. She gave me a quick glance and a nervous smile and went back to work.

Rath and Olds were behind the counter. Rath said, "Charlie, I think we ought to move out everybody that's workin' south of here before the same thing happens again."

Myers said, "They won't like it. Buffalo's thicker south than north."

Rath said, "If we don't move 'em out, the Indians will. They just might move this settlement out of here too."

Edith Clinger brought my dinner. I was hungry and began to eat. Rath said, "Maybe if we called a meeting for tonight. . . ."

"All of them ain't here."

"A lot of 'em are. Anderson Moore's here. I can speak for my two camps. Juan Santos came in before dawn with a load of hides, and the Mooars are due in before dark."

Myers nodded, "All right. Call the meeting. But I can't promise to get Hagerman to come in. You know how he is."

I didn't know whether I was relieved to hear that or not. I wanted to hunt buffalo, but I didn't much want to have to fight Indians to do it. I finished eating and mopped up the gravy on my plate with half a biscuit.

I went outside, thinking that it looked as if I had arrived here too late. If I'd got here a month ago, I'd probably have several hundred dollars earned by now. But I hadn't got here a month ago, and if the Indians drove these men from their hunting grounds, I'd have to go with them to Dodge. I could probably find something to do though, freighting, driving a coach, punching cows.

At about one-thirty, some men carried the bodies of Antelope Jack and Blue Billy out of Myers' store. They loaded them in the back of a wagon. Myers fired a shotgun and everybody in the settlement gathered for the burial. Neither O'Malley nor Westerhoff joined the crowd. They stayed at their wagon, guarding it.

Walking, everybody followed the wagon out to the two freshly dug graves. Myers read from his Bible and the bodies were lowered. Myers sprinkled a couple of handfuls of earth into each and the crowd dispersed. I picked up the shovel and began to fill them in.

Myers stayed behind and watched. When I stopped for breath, he asked, "Still want to hunt buffalo?"

I wasn't sure, but I said, "Sure."

"Even if Hagerman won't hunt north of here?"

I asked, "How many men has Hagerman got with him?"

"Three skinners. I figure to send another skinner along with you. That'll make six men in all."

I said, "There were twenty Indians in that bunch that attacked Plummer's camp."

Myers said, "It's up to you. You think on it and let me know."

I said, "I came here to hunt buffalo. Unless you know something I don't, I'll go down there just like I said I would." I looked straight at him as I said that.

He tried to meet my glance but he couldn't. He looked away, saying irritably, "What the hell do you mean by that?"

I said, "Amos Chapman didn't ride all this way just for his health."

Myers said, "They were hunting horse thieves. You heard what they said."

"Horse thieves way out here? The only horse thieves within a hundred miles are Indians."

Myers said, "All right. Chapman had some cock-and-bull story about Quanah Parker and some other chiefs having a pow-wow. How the hell he's supposed to have known about it, he didn't say. Anyway, he said they was going to attack this place."

"And you didn't want it to get out for fear everybody would leave?"

"That's it. Hell, there's enough men and enough firepower here to hold off the whole damn Comanche tribe, with the Kiowas thrown in. Maybe Chapman just wants us to leave so's he can move in with a bunch of hunters of his own."

The idea made sense. As much sense as that an Indian attack was really planned.

Myers started back, calling over his shoulder, "We'll head out to Hagerman's first thing in the morning."

I finished filling in the graves and mounded the earth over them. Several times I glanced toward the south. I didn't much like leaving here before Clinger arrived, but I'd come to hunt buffalo, not wait for him.

I wondered what would happen to Edith Clinger when her husband came. Would she agree to go back with him? I didn't think she would. But whether she'd be able to resist if he just took her by force was something else. Nor was it likely that any of the men at the settlement would intervene in her behalf. They were too used to minding their own business.

Westerhoff was at the bar in the saloon when I went in. There was a space on either side of him. One man was speaking as I went in. "Where'd you git that Injun gal? Is she Comanch or Kiowa? It's hard to tell, lookin' at her bare like that."

"She's Comanch."

"An' she's O'Malley's wife, you say?"

"White man fashion or Injun?"

"Well, they wasn't hitched up in a church, if that's what you mean."

"Married Injun fashion, then. O'Malley

must be pretty thick with the Comanch if they'd let him marry into the tribe like that."

"Hell, I didn't say he married into the tribe. He just took her. That's what the Injuns do."

I butted in and said, "Truth is, you and O'Malley kidnapped her. Ain't that the way it was?"

"So what if it was? You an Injun lover or somethin'?"

I said, "Not especially. I just know that somebody in the tribe took out on her trail when she was missed. They found where you picked her up. They found your horse tracks and that took 'em to your wagon tracks. They're likely out there right now, not more'n a mile from here, waitin' for their chance."

"What the hell do you think we ought to do?" Westerhoff asked. "Turn her loose? Let her go back to 'em and tell 'em all that's been done to her? They'd come in an' tear this goddamn place apart."

I said, "They know what's happened to her. They know what happens to a white woman when they catch her, and they don't figure we're any different from them."

Somebody asked, "Then you think they'll try and rescue her?"

I said, "I'm no Indian expert, but I'd say they would."

Westerhoff said, "Hell, they don't give a damn for their women. They trade 'em around like whores."

Myers said, "Now that's a goddamn lie. An Indian's as fussy about his women as a white man."

Westerhoff finished his drink. "Well, anyway, we got her an' we ain't turning her loose. And if you boys won't pay to crawl into the wagon with her, we'll just take her on north to Dodge." He stalked out of the saloon.

I finished my drink and went outside. Over by the corral, the two Mooars brothers, having just arrived, were hitching up empty wagons. One by one, the wagons pulled over to where the dry buffalo hides were piled. Men began tossing up the heavy hides to be stacked neatly and tramped down by other men on top.

I walked over to watch, staying to windward because of the stink. Every time a hide was lifted from the pile, hundreds of black bugs would scurry to get away. There was a cloud of flies over the piled-up hides, making a continuous buzzing sound.

So the Mooars were loading up, preparatory to pulling out for Dodge. I was willing to bet that sometime tomorrow, Myers and Rath would begin loading their hides too. It looked to me like the rats were leaving a sinking ship in spite of what Myers had told me earlier. If the Mooar brothers were leaving, it meant they, at least, had believed Chapman's story about an attack.

I got my gear together, saddle, blankets, slicker, and guns. I piled them beside Myers' store, where I'd slept previously. This way I'd be ready at dawn.

Edith Clinger came out and stood for a moment in front of Rath's store. She had plainly been working hard. Her hair was damp with perspiration and her sleeves were rolled up to her elbows. She stood there in the breeze for a few moments, cooling off, then turned to go back in. Seeing me, she changed her mind and came toward me.

She was very worried. It showed in her eyes. She said, "He should have been here before now."

I said, "Maybe he's not coming at all."

"Oh, he'll be coming all right." She saw the way I had piled my gear against the wall. "Are you leaving?" she asked worriedly.

I said, "I'm going to Hagerman's camp with Myers in the morning."

Her eyes had an almost panicky look to them. "Oh. I'd hoped. . . ." She stopped, made a determined smile, and said, "I guess I had hoped you would be here when he came."

"Why? It would only make things worse."

She did not reply to that. I asked, "What are you going to do? When he comes, I mean?"

She said firmly, "I am not going back with him."

"And if he forces you?"

"I'll kill him!" There was a fierce intensity in her voice.

All the swelling was gone from her face and the bruises had faded considerably. She was a pretty woman, I thought. There was a lot I liked about her, but she was Clinger's wife and I didn't intend to get in between.

Maybe it was a good thing I was leaving for Hagerman's camp tomorrow. If I was here when Clinger came, I'd probably end up squarely where I didn't want to be — between him and his wife. If he tried to beat her again, where I could see or hear, I wouldn't be able to stay out of it.

Edith Clinger said, "I may not see you again. If I don't, good-bye. And thank you for all you have done for me."

I nodded and watched her walk back toward Rath's. Her eyes were downcast and her shoulders slumped in a way that made me feel ashamed, even though I knew I had no cause to be.

Chapter 8

I was up half an hour before dawn, having been awakened by the moving around of Olds and his wife. I went out and got my horse, brought him back, and saddled him. I tied on my gear, then tied the horse in front of Myers' store.

I could smell coffee boiling in Rath's store, so I went in. Mrs. Olds was baking up a batch of sourdough biscuits. Olds was slicing buffalo hump into steaks. Edith Clinger was sitting on a stool, peeling potatoes and slicing them.

She got up and brought me a cup of coffee as soon as I sat down. Her eyes were worried, and for a moment I wished I wasn't going out to Hagerman's camp today.

Myers came in, rubbing sleep out of his eyes and running his hands through his tousled hair. He sat down and Mrs. Olds served us. Both of us ate quickly and without talk. Finished, we paid and left. I told Edith Clinger good-bye, trying not to see the frightened look in her eyes. Clinger must be a real bastard, I thought, for her to be so terribly afraid of him.

I helped Myers catch a team and hitch them to a wagon. Then I rode out beside the wagon as it took a rutted, two-track road heading south. I kept the new Sharps buffalo gun resting across the saddle in front of me, loaded in case there was need for it.

We crossed the Canadian, climbed the bluff beyond, and continued south. I saw the tracks of unshod ponies several times. Each time, I counted as best I could. I figured the largest bunch of Indians was about fifteen or twenty, the smallest about four.

On horseback, we could have reached Hagerman's camp in a couple of hours, or three. With the ponderous freight wagon, it took until noon.

The camp was on the bank of a narrow stream flowing north toward the Canadian. It was much like the other camp where I had seen Wallace and Dudley killed. Green hides were pegged out to dry, covering an acre or more of ground. Dry hides were stacked in the camp itself. A canvas was tied between three scrubby trees, providing shade from the sun and shelter from rain. The camp was deserted except for half a dozen wolves prowling its perimeter. They moved away as we approached, staying just out of effective rifle range.

I was disappointed that nobody was here. Myers pulled the wagon up beside one of the piles of dry hides. "Help me load," he said.

Even dry, a buffalo hide is heavy. Not only is it heavy, it's unwieldy and awkward. Myers got on one side of the pile, I got on the other, and we began tossing up the hides. Periodically, Myers and I would both climb up on top of the pile and tamp it down. The stink was almost unbearable. The sun was hot and there must have been a million flies buzzing around. They were so thick you didn't dare open your mouth. Finally I got the bandanna out of my pocket and tied it over my mouth and nose.

We had just about finished loading that particular pile when I heard a Sharps booming in the distance. I guessed the sound was over a mile away, but it was upwind, and that made it easier to hear. Myers said, "Sounds like he's got a stand. Wait until I unhitch one of these horses. We'll go take a look. I want you to see Hagerman at work."

He unhitched one of the horses, jumped to his back, and we rode out, heading toward the steady booming sound of Hagerman's Sharps. The horse that Myers had was big and wouldn't go faster than a trot, so it was half an hour before we reached the top of a low ridge from which we could look down and see Hagerman and his stand of buffalo.

He was on the other side of a wide grassy valley, on a slope beside a scattering of good-sized rocks. Beyond, at the crest of the ridge, I could see his horse, unconcernedly cropping grass.

The buffalo were between Hagerman and us. They were moving along the valley floor into the light breeze. The valley in front of Hagerman was littered with great, shaggy carcasses. Hagerman was squatting on his haunches, using a tripod to steady the gun. He would shoot and a buffalo would go down heavily. Those nearest the downed animal would bellow and paw the ground, and sometimes cluster around the dead buffalo. But they couldn't see Hagerman, and they couldn't smell him, and they didn't know where the danger was. They kept moving like a tide past the hunter on the slope, but only the smaller animals got safely past. The big bulls and cows went down. I didn't count, but I guessed that close to a hundred buffalo already lay on the ground, some kicking, most lying still.

Hagerman had two guns and, even from where we were, I could see the glitter of cartridges, both full and empty, lying on the ground beside him. He would use one gun until it was too hot to hold, then lay it aside and use the other one. I'd heard that buffalo hunters often urinated on their gun barrels to cool them during a stand. In Hagerman's case it wasn't necessary.

Myers said, "We'd just as well get down and wait. Unless something spooks the herd, this could go on all afternoon."

I dismounted and tied my horse out of sight below the crest of the ridge. Myers followed suit. Afterward, he moved carefully back and sat down to watch. I didn't know where Hagerman's skinners were. Probably out of sight the way we were, waiting for the killing to be over with.

The booming continued. Myers said, "You spot a herd poking along like this one is and you move down as close as you can get and set up your stand. As long as you don't move sideways, chances are you won't be seen because their eyesight is bad. Move straight toward them all the time and take it slow. Always be sure you're not upwind or in a position where a shift of wind will take your smell to them. If one of them starts to spook, kill that one quick or they'll all follow him. Best way is to kill the animals farthest away from you rather than those nearest you."

Suddenly, beyond Hagerman, on the crest of the ridge, a line of galloping Indians appeared. They were whooping shrilly, and immediately all the shaggy heads raised and turned toward them. There was an instant of immobility. Then the herd of buffalo began to move, gathering speed, stampeding down the valley into the wind.

Hagerman hesitated between the Indians and the buffalo. He apparently decided to stay with the buffalo. Completely ignoring the Indians after that, he methodically killed seven more big bulls before the last stragglers of the herd had thundered past.

He was now almost obscured by dust raised by the stampeding herd, but I saw him turn, reposition his tripod, and begin firing at the Indians. I made a quick count and came up with thirty-seven in the band. Hagerman hit one horse and the animal went down. The Indian leaped up behind one of his companions and the whole band disappeared below the crest of the ridge.

I looked at Myers. His eyes were worried but he didn't say anything. Thirty-seven was a hell of a lot of Indians. Even including Myers, there were only six of us.

We got our horses and rode down into the valley. I had not thought I would be affected by the slaughter of buffalo, but I had been

91

wrong. It was a shock to see so many of the huge, shaggy beasts lying there. Most had not yet completely shed their winter hair and it clung in lighter patches to their hides. A few were still kicking, and one raised his head and stared at us with reddened eyes.

Hagerman's three skinners came down the slope behind him, each driving a wagon. At the bottom of the hill they halted. One of them unhitched his team. The other two were already at work by the time it was done.

It was a thing of ruthless efficiency, and fascinating to watch. A few swift movements with their knives, and the legs were skinned. A chain was secured to the tail and the horse hitched to the chain. Seconds later the hide was off. It was cut loose at the neck, leaving a naked carcass with the shaggy head attached.

Hagerman was still on the hillside. Myers rode up to him and I followed. Myers had said he was bringing another skinner out today. I hadn't thought to ask him why he had not, but it was probably because no one had been willing to come, in view of the Indian scare.

Hagerman sat on the ground, knees up, his arms folded on his knees, and his head resting on his arms. He was as wet as if he had just come out of a river. When he glanced up, there was a look of utter exhaustion in his eyes.

Never could I remember seeing a man so tired. And suddenly I understood that his weariness was not altogether physical, hard as the work had been. So full of hate was he, that killing buffalo was a kind of fulfillment for that hate. He had exhausted himself the way a man will with a woman after months alone, and it had been an almost frantic thing that had left him drained.

Hagerman's eyes focused gradually on Myers and lost their look of utter weariness. He growled, "What are you doing here?"

"I brought you a hunter. His name is Burdett. Jess Burdett." He looked at me. "Jess, this is Herman Hagerman."

I didn't dismount because I didn't want to shake hands with Hagerman. You can't like a man who lives on hate. Hagerman scowled at me for several minutes without saying anything. Then he got wearily to his feet and began gathering up his gear. He carefully gathered all the empties and dropped them into one pocket of a ragged canvas coat. He dropped the live cartridges into the other pocket. He picked up the tripod and the two heavy rifles and trudged down the slope toward the wagons without looking back.

Myers glanced at me. "Know anything about skinning?"

I said, "No, but I sure as hell can learn."

We rode down and dismounted. We tied our horses and got knives from the dozen or so in a homemade leather rack on the back of one of the wagon seats.

Myers worked one side of a big buffalo bull and I worked the other. I watched the way he did it and then did it the same way myself. He was done with both legs before I was done with one.

Hagerman's skinner drove a horse over and Myers hitched him on. The horse pulled the hide loose, dragging the carcass several yards in the process. Myers said, "Cut it loose," and I did. Next time I got a carcass of my own and skinned out the legs without any help. Again the hide was yanked loose by a straining horse.

It was getting dark before we got through skinning the buffalo Hagerman had killed. But we weren't finished. The green hides, with blood streaming from them, had to be loaded and hauled back to camp. I was as exhausted as Hagerman had been by the time we arrived.

They had left some hump meat cooking in a pot over some coals when they rode out this morning, and it was ready now to eat.

The meat was tough and stringy despite cooking all day long, but it tasted as good as anything I've ever put into my mouth. The coffee was scalding, and there were some stale sourdough biscuits that someone had baked several days before.

Afterward we sat wearily around the fire. Two of the skinners had pipes. Hagerman and the other skinner bit off a chew. I lighted a cigar and offered Myers one, which he refused.

Hagerman said, "That was a lot of red-skins up there on the ridge. I counted thirty-seven of 'em. Anybody else had any trouble with the bastards, Charlie?"

Myers hesitated. I think he was considering telling Hagerman a lie. He probably decided against it only because he knew he couldn't get away with it. He said, "A little."

Hagerman looked at me. "What does he mean, a little? How can you have a little trouble with a goddamn Comanch?"

I said, "They killed Wallace and Dudley, and they got Holmes and Blue Billy too."

Hagerman stared across the fire at Myers. "A little trouble, you say?"

Myers said, "So be more careful. Don't let 'em catch you off your guard."

"That bunch this afternoon wouldn't have to catch us off guard. Hell, they coulda

95

rolled right over us."

Myers said, "They're scared of a buffalo gun. They've seen what a Sharps can do."

"Couldn't be that scared. Hell, they'd have galloped right over me before I could get more'n three."

Myers said, "Maybe they didn't want to give you three."

"Or maybe they're waitin' for somethin'," Hagerman said.

One of the skinners, a man named Gallegos, asked, "What would they be waitin' for?"

"How the hell should I know? More Injuns maybe. Or maybe they're waitin' for that murderin' renegade Quanah Parker hisself."

The skinner asked, "So what are we goin' to do?"

"Do? Hell we're goin' to keep on doin' what we been doin' all along. We come here to kill buffalo, an' that's what we're goin' to do."

The skinner said, "I don't know. Thirty-seven Indians is a lot, an' we don't even know that's all. A man'd be a'scairt to sleep."

Hagerman said, "We'll post a guard."

Gallegos said, "I don't know. What do you think, Mr. Myers?"

Myers hesitated. He plainly wanted to tell them there wasn't anything to worry about, but the thirty-seven Indians had scared him too. He said, "Might be better if you moved your camp up north of Adobe Walls, Hagerman. Could be they'll let you alone up there."

"Ain't so many buffalo north of the Canadian. Hell with you."

Gallegos said, "Mr. Hagerman, I'm goin' in. I don't know what good a few more dollars is goin' to be to me if I lose my scalp."

The other two skinners agreed. Hagerman looked at me. "What about you?"

I said, "I can't skin all the buffalo you can kill by myself. And I sure as hell ain't going to stay if everybody else pulls out."

Scowling, Hagerman got up and stamped off into the darkness, muttering to himself.

Chapter 9

Hagerman was up most of the night, pacing back and forth. Occasionally, when I was awake myself, I would hear him curse.

It might be a good thing for him if he had to stop killing buffalo, I thought. He was half out of his mind with hatred for the Indians, and I didn't suppose I could blame him much. But living on hate isn't good for anyone. And on top of that, if you live by killing, and killing, and more killing, it's liable to warp you for the rest of your life.

Myers roused the camp an hour before dawn. We got up and took positions behind the loaded hide wagons, waiting for dawn, when an attack was most likely. Hagerman had both his Sharps. He had a hundred or so cartridges on the ground beside him, just as if he had a stand of buffalo. I was fairly close to him and I could feel the tension in the man. He was trembling all over, not like a man who is cold or afraid, but like a hound on a leash, waiting for the command to go, trembling with eagerness.

The sky began to pale. For a little while a

breeze blew out of the east, fresh with the smell of grass and sage and of hundreds of miles of emptiness. When it died, the old gagging stink of death was here, and I knew suddenly that, money or no, I couldn't do it. Not day after day, the way Hagerman did. I couldn't wallow in blood and death, and breathe the smell of death, and live with it on my clothes and hands. I had fooled myself. As soon as possible, I would ride north to Dodge and get myself a job doing something else.

With that decision made, I was anxious to get going, to get back to Adobe Walls. The Mooars, and Myers and Rath, had a wagon train of hides going north, probably today. I could go with them and get this stink out of my nostrils once and for all.

It was now light enough to see the surrounding hillsides, but there were no Indians. Birds began to chirp their welcome to the dawn. The ever-present wolves prowled the perimeter of the camp, making me wonder how many wolves there were where Hagerman's stand had been. Dozens probably. The abundance of food must have drawn wolves from a hundred miles away, by that strange instinct animals possess, the instinct that draws buzzards for miles when a single animal lies dead upon the plain.

The sun poked above the horizon in the east and Myers got to his feet. He said, "Nothing's going to happen. Let's load up and get back to Adobe Walls."

There still were hides to load, but not all of them could be loaded. Some would have to be left behind and returned for later. But we worked for a couple of hours, piling dry hides as high as possible on the wagons. When everything was finally loaded and tied down, the wagons creaked away along the rutted road leading north. Myers drove one of them, Hagerman another. Two of the skinners drove the other two and the third skinner rode with me, off to the side. I kept watching the skyline for Indians, but I didn't see any, and that puzzled me. Why had they so suddenly disappeared?

The loaded wagons were top-heavy and cumbersome, and we had trouble getting them down into the Canadian and across without upsetting them. But finally they toiled up the bluff north of the river and around noon we reached Adobe Walls.

The wagons drew up in a line north of the buildings and the teams were unhitched. The men washed and headed for the restaurant.

I looked around carefully, but I didn't see any strangers. I didn't see Edith Clinger, either, but just as I reached the front door of Rath's store, she came stumbling out of it, almost falling in the dust. Behind her came a man, a scowling, powerful hulk of a man. He paid no attention to me, but grabbed her by an arm and yanked her to her feet.

He was about the same height as I, but was heavier and, except for a slight paunch, you couldn't say he had gone to fat. I had wondered what Edith had seen in so brutal a man that would make her marry him, but I hadn't seen him then. He was a handsome man, if he'd quit scowling, and he must have put himself out to be agreeable when he was courting her. Men seldom let their worst side show when they're looking for a wife.

Immediately behind Clinger came Mrs. Olds, a heavy cast-iron skillet in her hand. She made a run for him, swinging the skillet and cursing him in words I'd never heard any woman use. Clinger avoided the skillet and, without letting go of Edith, seized it and wrenched it out of her hand.

She went for his face, maybe to claw it, and Clinger let go of Edith and dropped the skillet. He bawled, "You damn she-wolf, get away from me or I'll give you what your husband got!"

He caught both her wrists. Olds came from the store now, a shotgun in his hands.

His face was a mess, mouth smashed, nose streaming blood. There was a swelling the size of a walnut on his cheekbone, and one of his eyes was already turning black. He walked in a painful, twisted way that said broken ribs to me. But he could talk. He hobbled to Clinger and jammed the shotgun into his side. "Let go of her, you son-of-a-bitch, or I'll blow a hole in you big enough to drive a wagon through!"

Clinger froze momentarily. Then he let go of Mrs. Olds who, sobered now, backed off. Olds said, "Get your horse and get out of here! Next time I see you I'll kill you!"

Clinger carefully backed away from the shotgun. He reached for his wife again.

What had happened was plain enough. Olds had tried to keep Clinger from taking Edith and had gotten badly beaten for his pains. The other men, who had crowded out of Rath's, stood staring, not offering to intervene.

Edith's eyes met mine briefly. Resolutely she looked away. I said, "Clinger!"

He swung his shaggy head. "Who the hell are you?"

I said, "The one you're looking for, I expect. Jess Burdett."

"So you're the son-of-a-bitch!"

I said, "I'm the son-of-a-bitch. Now turn

102

loose of her because I'm going to give you a little of what you been givin' her."

He stood still for a minute or so, sizing me up, and that was in character, I thought. A man that beats women don't like getting beat himself, and he don't care much for a fair fight where he hasn't got any advantage on his side.

I said, as nastily as I could, "Beating me ain't going to be quite as easy as beating your wife, Clinger. You sure you've got the stomach for it?" He was big enough so that I knew he'd be a match for me. He was heavier, and as tall, and I had the feeling if one of his big fists connected it would hurt. I figured one way to make him reckless was to get him mad.

He growled deep in his throat like an animal. I said, "That might scare women but it don't scare me. You going to fight or not?"

Edith burst in now, grabbing her husband's arm and saying, "I'll go with you. Just let him alone."

He turned his head and snarled, "Scared I'll mark his pretty face, you goddamn whore?"

I saw her face go white, as if he had slapped it physically. And I didn't see why either she or I should have to take any more of his abuse. I took the fight to him, letting him have a long, looping right, squarely on the nose.

It burst like a ripe tomato, and squirted blood all over his face and shirtfront. He let go of Edith and she scurried to get out of the way. I hadn't staggered him, I had only stung him. With a rumbling roar he rushed at me.

I stumbled on a stick of firewood someone had left lying on the ground, and was off balance for an instant. It was enough for Clinger. Before I could set myself again, he struck me a blow that skidded off the point of my chin and caught me squarely in the throat.

By God, I've never felt anything like that. My throat closed like a rock had been jammed down into it. I couldn't get any air, I couldn't breathe out, and the pain was like nothing I've ever felt before. I forgot all about Clinger, forgot about Edith and the fight. All I could think was that if I didn't get some air I was going to die. Gasping and choking and clawing at my throat, I went to the ground.

I might have forgotten Clinger but he sure hadn't forgotten me. Out of the corner of my eye I saw him coming, aiming a vicious kick that caught me squarely in the ribs.

It must have broken several. I felt like I

had a fire burning inside my chest. Still choking for air, I rolled and tried to protect myself. I caught a second kick, this one landing on my back. I've been in a few tight spots in my life, but suddenly I knew this was the worst. Nobody was going to interfere. It wasn't their way. And, if nobody intervened, Clinger was going to kick me to death with his heavy boots.

Each kick that landed meant I had less chance of ever getting up. I suppose I knew that instinctively. Instinct also brought me fighting to my hands and knees. I had managed to suck a little air into my lungs, though it went in whistling, and I had managed to exhale part of it. I took another kick in the same ribs that had taken the first one, and the pain was so excruciating it must have cleared my head. On hands and knees already, I came up, lunging forward, trying to drive my head into Clinger's paunch, which I sensed would be the place he could most easily be hurt.

He was coming at me and didn't expect any more resistance out of me. So he was unprotected, and what muscles he had in his belly were relaxed. I struck him, my momentum combining with his to give the blow a force it would not otherwise have had. It drove a huge gust of air from him and, Myers, watching, told me later that his face twisted as if he had been hurt pretty bad.

As for me, I wasn't even seeing very well. My lungs were laboring, trying to inhale and exhale through my collapsed windpipe. My ribs were an area of blinding pain. I didn't know who I was fighting or why. I was suddenly an animal trying to survive.

Hurt, Clinger stepped back, bent half double, hugging his belly. I must have got him in that area just above the belly and just below the breastbone, where a man can be hurt so quickly and so easily. I looped a long right at him again, catching him squarely in the mouth. I felt teeth give before the blow, and heard them, and I felt a kind of savage joy as I suddenly remembered who this man was and why I was fighting him. I let him have a left that caught him in the eye, and a right again that missed partly but almost tore an ear from him.

He was recovering now from the belly blow just as I had recovered from his blow to my throat. For a few minutes, I don't know how many, we stood toe to toe, slugging it out, trading punch for punch. My own nose was smashed, my mouth bloodied, but I didn't care any more for the punishment I took. All I wanted to do was to mark him the way he had marked Edith, here in front of everybody.

How long we stood this way, giving punch for punch, I couldn't have said. But suddenly I became aware that I was no longer on my feet. Nor was he. We were on our knees, still slugging, though feebly now. It was effort just to raise my fist, even more of an effort to throw a punch. I didn't realize it, and I don't suppose he did, either, but we were both moving slowly and sluggishly. Where before we had each landed a dozen blows, we now were landing only one. And more punches missed than struck. Close to exhaustion, only hatred kept us fighting at all.

I heard someone yell, "Stop 'em," and heard another voice say, "Hell no, let 'em finish it. Let's see which one of the bastards wins."

I don't know where Clinger was trying to land his blows, and I didn't feel very many of them. But I knew where I was aiming mine. At his face. I wanted his goddamn face to look like ground meat when I was through with it.

And it did. Even through the haze that hung over my eyes I could see the blood that covered every part of his face. The man was no longer recognizable. Both his eyes were swelled nearly shut. His nose was flattened and bloodied. His cheekbones and jaw-bones had lumps and welts on them and his mouth was nothing but a bloody pulp. Every now and then he would spit blood as though still trying to spit out the broken teeth he'd gotten rid of a long time ago.

I fell, and a curtain of darkness descended. I wanted to lie there and sleep, to let go, to quit trying, but something wouldn't let me. I struggled up again, swinging blindly, missing but swinging anyway.

I fell over something, and clawed back to find out what it was. It was Clinger, and he didn't move.

Pushing against him, I struggled to my feet. I staggered, tried to straighten out, and staggered again. I was more thirsty than ever before in my life, and I croaked, "Water. Water."

Hands took hold of me. I was steered to the corral and my head was stuck under the spout of the pump. I let it run over my head and neck a while, then turned my face upward and gulped it thirstily.

Someone said, "Take him into my store. There's a mattress in the back. He ain't going to do nothing but sleep until tomorrow."

There was more movement, then semi-darkness, and finally the softness of a grass mattress under me. And everything turned black.

Chapter 10

I must have been beaten even worse than I had thought because I didn't awake until noon on the day following. When I did, it was to an awareness of pain in every part of my body. One of my eyes was swelled almost completely shut. My mouth was smashed. My body was one great big ache.

While I was out, my clothes had been removed. My midsection was tightly bandaged to hold the broken ribs in place. The dirt had been washed off of me. Even the way I hurt, I could still feel hot and embarrassed, wondering who had done it. Edith Clinger, I supposed, helped by Mrs. Olds.

I struggled to sit up, and groaned when the pain stabbed through me. Myers, working behind the counter, turned his head. "You awake? For a while there, I thought that you was dead." He brought me my clothes. They had been washed.

I struggled to my feet, wincing with every movement that I made. "I guess I damn near was. How about Clinger?"

Myers shrugged. "I guess that son-of-a-bitch is still out."

"Where is he?"

"Layin' out there in an empty wagon. Them two women took care of him an' threw a blanket over him, though I'm damned if I know why."

I put on my clothes and staggered to the front of the store. I went out into the blinding noonday sunlight. The first thing I noticed was that all the wagons were gone, those belonging to the Mooars brothers as well as those belonging to Myers and to Rath.

I had wanted to go with them, but it was too late now. Besides, I couldn't have ridden a horse and I couldn't have stood the jolting motion of a hide wagon all the way to Dodge. I still couldn't. Any ideas I'd had of leaving here would have to be changed. I'd have to stay for a few more days at least.

I staggered to Hanrahan's and went inside. My stomach was empty, but I wanted a drink before I ate. I went up to the bar, trying to walk as if I didn't hurt. I probably didn't fool anybody. Hanrahan was behind the bar and I said, "Whiskey." He set a bottle and glass in front of me and I dumped enough in the glass to fill it halfway to the top. I gulped it, hoping it would dull the pain.

Hanrahan peered at me. "Damn good fight you two put on," he said. "You should 'ave charged the boys a couple dollars each to watch."

I said, "Didn't think of it."

"If you fight him again, you let me handle it," said Hanrahan. "I'll make us all a few dollars out of it."

I poured myself another drink and downed that too. I asked, "When did the Mooars pull out?"

"This mornin', early. Took every wagon they had an' every hide they could pile onto 'em."

"How about Myers' and Rath's wagons?"

"Left with the Mooars."

"Rath go with 'em?"

"Uh uh. He an' Myers stayed."

I asked, "They going later?"

He peered closely at me as if wondering what had prompted me to ask. Then he shook his head. "They say not," he said.

I gulped the second drink. "How about you?" I asked.

"Me? Why would I want to leave? I ain't got no hides to be hauled to Dodge. My business is here, sellin' red-eye." But he didn't look at me, and I felt more sure than ever that Chapman had brought a warning and had conveyed it only to the five men who had built this post.

Still, if they had believed Chapman, it looked like Myers, Rath, and Hanrahan would also have left. Shrugging, I left the saloon and went next door to Rath's.

Edith Clinger glanced up as I came in. Her eyes lighted in a way that made me feel warm inside. I sat down and she said, "How do you feel?"

I grinned at her. "Sore."

She said, "I'm sorry."

"No need. I'll get over it."

"I mean I'm sorry I got you into it."

I said, "It was something I wouldn't have missed."

"It will keep you from hunting for a while, won't it?"

"I'd given up the idea of hunting."

She looked at me strangely, started to say something, then changed her mind. She asked, "Are you hungry?"

"I sure am. I can even eat buffalo hump and fried spuds."

"Good, because that happens to be just what we have." She filled a plate and put it in front of me. She filled a tin cup with coffee and brought that too. I sipped it even though it hurt my mouth.

Most of the men had left the restaurant. Olds came over and stood beside Edith. He asked, "Feeling better?"

I grinned. "You know how I feel. You took your lumps from Clinger too."

He nodded. "But I didn't take as much of it as you did. He quit on me after he'd knocked me down a couple of times."

I looked at Edith. "You're not going back with him, are you?"

She shook her head. "Not if I can help it. But you saw how he is."

I said, "Maybe he won't try forcing you to go a second time." She nodded, but she didn't believe it and neither did I. Furthermore, I knew that next time Clinger wouldn't try stopping me with his fists. If I stood in his way again, he'd try to kill me. And I was willing to bet he'd shoot me in the back if there wasn't any other way.

It took me a long time to eat because my mouth was so sore. It was early afternoon when I finished and went outside. Edith Clinger, Olds, and his wife stayed behind, cleaning up.

There were more men here than there had been yesterday. More hunters had come in, probably having heard about the deaths of Wallace, Dudley, Holmes, and Blue Billy. I guessed there must be over thirty here. And thirty, as well armed as these men were, could hold off a lot of Indians. Unless the

Indians took them by surprise.

Several men were standing beside an empty wagon looking into it. It was not a big hide wagon, but a smaller one, the kind used by overland travelers. They saw me watching and left the wagon. Grinning, they stopped in front of me. One of them said, "You ought to see how the other fella looks."

I said, "He couldn't feel a hell of a lot worse than I do."

"Maybe not, but he sure looks worse. Ain't come to yet, either."

I asked, "He's all right, isn't he?"

"He's breathin', if that's what you mean. That son-of-a-bitch is too damn mean to die."

They went into Hanrahan's saloon. I stood for a moment, soaking up the heat of the sun. All I really wanted to do was sleep, and there didn't seem to be any reason why I shouldn't. I went back into Myers' store and headed for the mattress where I'd spent last night.

Myers was behind the rough-hewed counter at the rear of the store. He was counting his money. When he got through, he put it into a leather sack. He put the sack under the counter.

I didn't think much of it at the time. I went to the mattress and lay down on it. I was almost instantly asleep.

When I awoke again the store was dark. Enough light from the stars came through the cracks between the upright pickets for me to see where things were. Light was coming from the doorway of Hanrahan's, so I knew it was not yet very late.

I got up, pleased to discover I was less sore than I had been earlier. I pulled on my boots and ran my fingers through my hair. I picked my way to the door through the piles of merchandise. There was also a light in Rath's.

I wasn't hungry and I didn't want a drink. I did want water, though, so I headed for the pump inside the corral.

Almost there, I caught a glimpse of someone crossing the open ground between the buildings and the wagon where O'Malley and Westerhoff kept the Indian girl. I looked more closely and saw that the figure was unmistakably that of a woman.

And it wasn't Mrs. Olds. The figure was too slight. It had to be Edith Clinger. It could be no one else.

I hurried after her and caught her before she reached the rear of O'Malley's wagon. I grabbed her arm. "What the hell do you think you're doing?" I whispered.

She was trembling and scared, but her

voice was determined. "I'm going to release that Indian girl."

I dragged her away from the wagon. I could smell tobacco smoke, so I knew the wagon was guarded. When we were far enough away to talk without being overheard, I said, "You're crazy. You can't let her go."

"Why not? I was going to slit the canvas and go in and cut her loose."

"She'd take the knife away from you and kill you with it."

"I don't think she would. She wouldn't attack me for helping her."

"You've got no right. . . ." I stopped. Talk wasn't going to stop Edith now that she'd come this far. I said, "All right. Suppose you do cut her loose? What then? What will you do with her?"

She showed me a bundle. "I have some clothes for her. I'm going to let her go."

"She'll go right back to her tribe. She'll tell them what's been done to her."

"Do you think she has not been missed?"

"It's crazy."

She said, "Jess, I know what it is like to be held against your will."

I said, "I won't help you."

"I didn't ask you to. I am quite capable. . . ."

I said, "Oh hell, all right. Give me the knife. You stay out of sight."

She put her hand on my arm and squeezed. I left her and walked to the front of the wagon. The guard was sitting there, his back against the wagon tongue. I could smell the smoke of his pipe more strongly. He got up. "Want to crawl in with that there Injun gal?" The voice sounded like that of Westerhoff. He couldn't see well enough to tell who I was, and that was the way I wanted it. I swung hard and caught him on the side of the jaw. My knuckles were already skinned and sore and I thought the blow must have hurt me as much as it hurt him. His pipe went flying, scattering sparks, and he went back, tripping over the wagon tongue and landing on his back. I went after him, prepared to hit him again, but it wasn't necessary. I must have caught him just right. He was out cold.

I called to Edith and she came hurrying to me. I handed her the knife. I said, "Cut her hands loose last. And be careful she don't get the knife away from you."

I knew if I went in I'd probably have to struggle with the Indian girl. And Edith just might be right. The girl might not fight her when she understood why she had come.

I heard Edith talking reassuringly to the

girl. The girl could not, of course, understand the words but she could understand the tone. A few moments later Edith came climbing out again. Behind her came the Indian girl, wearing the dress that Edith had taken in to her. Seeing me she stiffened and turned to run, only to fall sprawling on the ground. Frantically she began to crawl.

Edith went after her. She stopped her and talked to her some more in a whisper. The girl calmed and I was able to approach. Edith said, "What are we going to do? She can't walk. Her feet have been tied too long. Her ankles are raw from trying to pull loose."

There was only one place the girl could go, only one person who would help hide her from O'Malley and Westerhoff. That was Mrs. Olds. I said, "Take her to Rath's. Maybe you and Mrs. Olds can hide her until she can travel."

"How about a horse? She could probably ride."

I said, "I helped you get her loose, but I'll be damned if I'm going to steal a horse for her. She'll be able to travel by tomorrow."

"She can't leave in daylight."

"Then keep her hidden until tomorrow night." I was irritated at having been brought into this, and I knew it would be foolish to let the Indian girl escape.

Edith helped the girl toward Rath's store, almost carrying her. The girl must have been in great pain, but she never made a sound.

While Edith and the girl waited in the shadows. I went in to make sure no one except Olds and his wife were there. I beckoned to Edith and she helped the girl inside. I closed the door and stood in front of it so that nobody would surprise them by going in.

There'd be a hell of a commotion when O'Malley and Westerhoff discovered the girl was gone. Furthermore, they would know exactly where to look. Sourly, I thought that it wasn't enough to have Clinger to reckon with. I had to have O'Malley and Westerhoff too.

If I had any sense I'd mind my own business the way everyone else here did. Trouble was, I'd never had any sense.

Chapter 11

I didn't even have to wait for morning for the explosion out at O'Malley's wagon. Westerhoff came to less than an hour after I slugged him. He raised up yelling like he was being killed. Men came running, half awake, from Hanrahan's saloon. Westerhoff yelled, "Some son-of-a-bitch slugged me an' took the Injun gal!"

I suppose it was immediately obvious to everyone that the girl hadn't been stolen by somebody who wanted her for himself. The only reason for taking her would be to release her and save her from further debasement. And that conclusion pointed the finger straight at Mrs. Olds and Edith Clinger, both of whom had objected to the way the girl was being used.

O'Malley and Westerhoff came stalking over to Rath's store with a dozen or so men following. They streamed inside, demanding that Rath and Olds and the two women release the girl to them.

I got in behind maybe half a dozen others. Olds, his wife, and Edith Clinger stood behind the counter at the rear of the store. A single lantern burned, illuminating the scene. Edith Clinger had her old shotgun. Olds had another. O'Malley said angrily, "Give her back, ye thieves. She's ours, just as sure as the stuff behind the counter there is yours."

I could see Rath standing to one side. He knew he was going to have to take a stand, one way or the other, but he didn't want to antagonize the hunters and skinners and lose their business trying to save an Indian girl who meant nothing to him.

I'd helped Edith rescue the Indian girl, so there wasn't any doubt in my mind as to what I had to do. I stepped over behind the counter beside her and faced the crowd. I said, "You've lost her, O'Malley, same way the Indians lost her when you kidnapped her. Unless you're ready to take her back by force, why just get the hell out of here and let these folks alone."

O'Malley looked around at the other men, most of whom were only half awake and half dressed. None of them had guns. Knowing he'd get no help from them, O'Malley scowled. "Ye'll be sorry, ye son-of-a-bitch. I'll finish what Clinger started on ye."

He made me mad, so I mocked his Irish

brogue. "Ye do that, ye Irish bastard. If ye think ye're up to it." I knew I was in no shape to fight anyone, and O'Malley knew it too.

Growling, the pair backed out of the store. Rath looked relieved because he hadn't needed to interfere. When they all had gone, he looked at me and said, "That was pretty stupid. What the hell are you going to do with her?"

Edith said, "We're going to let her go. As soon as she's able to walk."

Rath grunted disgustedly and went back to his bed. Edith Clinger looked at me. "Thank you, Mr. Burdett."

I thought what a damn fool her husband was. He had a good woman, and a pretty one. He had a ranch and cattle, but he had something boiling inside of him so that none of it had any value for him. He took out his anger on her, and beat her and drove her away from him. I said, "It's all right," and walked away. The thoughts I was having then were thoughts no man should have about another's wife.

It took me a long time to go to sleep. When I awoke, the sun was already up. I pulled on my boots and washed at the pump in the corral. I then went out and moved my horse, which I still picketed in preference to turning him in with the horse herd.

Two wagons came in from the south, piled high with hides. The men drew them up beside the corral, unharnessed, turned the horses loose, then headed for the saloon. One man stayed behind, careful to stay out of sight behind the wagons. I couldn't see him well enough to tell what he looked like, but his actions were furtive. I was willing to bet he was the fugitive, Curt DeValois, that the bounty hunter, Argo, was looking for.

I'd stuck my nose into enough things that weren't my business to last me a while, and I made up my mind I'd keep it out of this. I went into Rath's for breakfast. The Indian girl, dressed in some of Mrs. Olds' clothes, which fit her like a tent, was sitting by the stove, rubbing her feet with her hands.

Edith brought my breakfast. Seeing me looking at the Indian girl, she said, "She's better. She can travel if we can find a way to get her away without her being seen."

I said, "You'll have to wait for night. If you let her go in daylight, O'Malley and Westerhoff will catch her again."

"I suppose you're right."

I asked, "Where's your husband?"

"I saw him down at the stream when I got up this morning. I haven't seen him since."

Argo, the bounty hunter, was sitting at the

end of the counter, just finishing up. He didn't speak to me and I didn't speak to him. I figured he'd check out the two newly arrived wagons soon enough without any urging from me.

When I went out, Rath was putting the money out of the cash drawer into a leather bag. I remembered that Myers had been doing the same thing yesterday, and I wondered if there was any connection. I suspected there was. Both Myers and Rath had sent their hide wagons north with the Mooars brothers. Chances were, both would be following by horseback today. They could catch the wagons fifteen or twenty miles north of here.

If they left, I'd be sure in my own mind, at least, that Amos Chapman had brought a warning of an impending attack.

Argo went out and I followed him. I had one cigar left, nearly shredded from being struck by one of Clinger's fists. I licked it enough to stick it back together again and lighted it. Argo stood for a moment, staring at the newly arrived wagons. Then he crossed toward them.

He was still fifty yards away when a shot racketed. Smoke billowed from beneath one of the wagons.

Argo didn't hesitate. He broke into an instant run, dodging back and forth as he ran to throw off the ambusher's aim.

If there had been any doubt that the man hiding behind the wagons was DeValois, it now was gone. Zigzagging, Argo reached the wagons and dodged behind one of them.

He threw himself to his belly, shoving his rifle out ahead. But he didn't shoot.

I was a little puzzled by that. The reward would be paid for DeValois, dead or alive. And for the first time it occurred to me that Argo might be more than just a bounty hunter. He might possibly have a personal stake in the capture of DeValois.

DeValois kept shooting at the wagon beneath which Argo had hidden himself. I counted the shots, as he showed himself just enough to draw the fire of the man behind the other wagon.

Originally, one shot had been fired. Argo drew the others, one by one. When five in all had been fired, he leaped recklessly to his feet and sprinted for the hide wagon behind which DeValois was concealed.

He was taking a tremendous risk, more risk than a man would take for a few hundred dollars, unless he was a fool. He didn't know whether DeValois had a rifle in addition to the revolver he had just emptied at him. Nor did he know if DeValois had an extra cylinder for the revolver, which he could slip into place in seconds and begin firing again.

But no more shots came. Argo plunged beneath the hide wagon, sliding, propelled by the speed at which he had been running. He slid a full ten feet, all the way under the wagon. On the other side, DeValois got up and ran.

Argo clawed to his feet and took after him. About twenty-five feet separated the two, but Argo closed it fast. Almost to the horse herd before he caught DeValois, he made a diving catch, and brought him crashing to the ground.

Deliberately now, Argo let DeValois get to his feet. DeValois turned to run again, and once more Argo brought him crashing to the ground.

This time, DeValois came up with a rock fisted in his hand. The two circled each other warily for a moment. Then Argo rushed, furiously, like someone who couldn't wait.

DeValois swung the rock, but Argo ducked and it missed. Argo caught DeValois's arm, whirled, bringing the arm over his shoulder. Turning, he bent forward, throwing DeValois bodily over his head to land some ten or twelve feet away. But he did something else, too, as DeValois's scream of pain testified. He broke DeValois's arm.

DeValois lay writhing on the ground, but Argo wasn't finished yet. He ran to the downed man and kicked him savagely, squarely in the face. DeValois rolled, bringing up his knees to protect himself, and Argo kicked him in the back with what seemed like enough force to snap his spine.

Now, suddenly, DeValois seemed to realize that to stay down was to be kicked to death. He clawed to his feet. Apparently realizing that no safety lay out beyond the post, he turned and ran straight back toward us, broken arm held steady with his good hand, shuffling, and in pain.

Argo was right behind him, faster and unhurt. But he didn't catch him, even though doing so would have been easy for him. He let DeValois cross the creek, let him stumble right to where we were, a crowd of perhaps twenty men watching what was going on.

DeValois, out of breath and nearly blind with pain, fell on his knees half a dozen yards away from us. "For God's sake," he begged. "Don't let him kill me! Any man's entitled to a trial!"

Argo came up right behind him. He said, between clenched teeth, "Not you, you son-of-a-bitch."

Myers said, "I thought you was takin' him to Dodge for the reward."

Argo, standing over DeValois, said, "I am. But the posters say dead or alive."

Myers said, "Let 'im alone. He's beat. All you got to do now is tie him up."

Argo turned his glance on Myers. His face was white, almost gray. His mouth was a thin line. His eyes were sunken in his head, but they almost seemed to glow. He said furiously, "You want to stop me, you son-of-a-bitch?"

Myers stared at him for a moment more. I think he knew, in that instant, that there was more to this than a bounty hunter taking a prisoner. He closed his mouth and kept it closed.

Argo kicked DeValois once more, squarely in the face. I could hear teeth snap, and maybe other bones as well. DeValois covered his face with his hands. Argo kicked him again in the back, squarely on the lower spine.

The pain of this made DeValois roll, made him come to his hands and knees, apparently with the intention of trying to defend himself. Argo swung his heavy boot. Once more it caught DeValois squarely in the face.

Three savage kicks had changed his face

to a mess of mangled meat. All his front teeth were gone, broken off at the gums. His nose, flattened and broken three times, was a shapeless, bruised, and bloody mess. Both his eyes were swelled nearly shut. His jaw was slack, probably broken on both sides. If he ever recovered, it would be a miracle.

His arm was broken and his spine must be injured, or broken, because his legs apparently were paralyzed. Argo swung his changed and twisted face toward me. "Saddle my horse and his."

I shook my head. "Saddle 'em yourself."

He raised his gun and for a moment I thought he was going to shoot. Myers broke in. "Put that damn thing down! You want horses, you saddle 'em."

Argo stood there over DeValois's broken body, his chest heaving with his effort to draw air into his starving lungs. He said, speaking jerkily because of his breathlessness, "Maybe you want to know why. Well — by God I'll — tell you why. He killed a girl all right, and there's a bounty out on him. Know who put the bounty up? Me. Because it was my girl he killed."

There was a long silence after that. Mrs. Olds and Edith Clinger had come out of Rath's. They stood there, shocked and white-faced, for once at a loss for words. At last Myers said, "You ain't got much chance of making it all by yourself."

Argo said, "I'll try."

Myers said, "If the Injuns kill him, he ain't goin' to hang. An' if they kill you, you ain't goin' to see him hang."

I said, "Ain't no doctor here. Longer he lays here hurt, the longer he's goin' to pay for what he done."

Argo finally nodded reluctantly. Mrs. Olds came forward and Rath said, "Find a bed for him someplace. Put him in the wagon where Clinger was. I don't want him in my store."

Several men came forward and lifted DeValois, who screamed with the pain as they did. They carried him toward the wagon where Clinger had been, with Mrs. Olds and Edith Clinger following.

Argo seemed drained of strength. And I had to admit I felt a lot different about him than I had before. I said, "Come on into Hanrahan's and I'll buy you a drink." I caught a glimpse of Karl Lutz's face as we headed for the saloon. He couldn't meet my glance and quickly looked away.

Chapter 12

All morning there was an air of expectancy at the post at Adobe Walls. Practically all the big hide wagons had gone, headed for Dodge, and with them had gone a sizable number of men at the post. New arrivals had, however, kept the complement about the same. I guessed there must still be about thirty men here.

It was the trouble here in the settlement more than the Indian trouble, I told myself, that made everybody so damned edgy and irritable. First there had been Clinger and the fight he'd had with me, as well as the beating he'd given Olds. Then there had been O'Malley and Westerhoff and the captive Indian girl. Thirdly, there had been the vicious fight between Argo and DeValois. I suppose everybody was wondering what was going to happen next.

Coming out of the saloon near noon, I passed Clinger coming in. I have to admit that I got considerable pleasure out of seeing the damage I'd done to his face. He kept his mouth closed, but blood still drooled from both corners, evidence of broken teeth. His mouth was smashed and scabbed. Both eyes were swelled nearly shut. His nose was flattened and broken, and there were still plenty of bruises elsewhere on his face. He glowered at me and I made myself grin at him. That only made his stare more murderous. I knew immediately that I'd been a fool to mock the man. I was only feeding the flames of hatred in him, and already they were murderous enough.

Clinger was capable of shooting me in the back, or of shooting me from ambush and, if Indians did attack this post, he'd use the attack as an excuse to kill me the instant he could get me in his sights.

I went over to Rath's. I sat down at the counter. As usual, Edith Clinger, Olds, and Mrs. Olds were working behind it, getting the noon meal ready. I didn't see the Indian girl. When Edith brought me a tin cup of coffee, I asked, "How's she getting along?"

"Fair. She's been through a lot. If she wasn't so tough, she'd already be dead. They had her tied hand and foot most of the night. And besides selling her to everyone that wanted her, they beat her and starved her, and I guess they didn't give her any water at all."

She left me, and a few moments later came back with my dinner. Other men were coming in now. Before I had finished, the counter was full. I went outside and headed for Myers' store to buy some cigars.

Just before I went in the door, something made me look toward the north. About a quarter mile away, just entering the timber, I saw two horsemen. They were a long ways off, but I recognized them anyway. One was Charlie Myers. The other was Charlie Rath.

Then I had been right. The news they'd received from Amos Chapman had been a warning of an Indian attack. They'd shipped their hides north with the Mooars brothers, claiming they themselves were going to stay. But they had lied. They were leaving the sinking ship like rats, without even bothering to tell those left behind what they were probably going to be up against.

I turned and went into the saloon. Only two men were at the bar, and Hanrahan was behind it. The two men finished their drinks and left, leaving Hanrahan and me alone. I said, "Myers and Rath just rode out."

He nodded. "I know it."

"How come you didn't go with them? Chapman told you about the attack just like he told Myers and Rath."

Hanrahan nodded.

"Then why ain't you skedaddling?"

He said, "Chapman said the attack was supposed to be on June 27th. He was sure of that. June 27th, he said."

I said, "That's tomorrow."

Hanrahan nodded.

I asked, "How the hell could they know the exact date, for God's sake?"

He said, "That's what made it sound so damn fishy to me. I figure the Army sent Chapman with that warning just to get us to pick up and leave this place. Or else Chapman is acting for a bunch that plan to move in here just as soon as we pull out."

I said, "Myers and Rath and the Mooars must have believed what he said."

Hanrahan grinned. "They're just playing it safe. They want to get their hides to Dodge anyhow, before the market's glutted and the price goes down."

"So what are you going to do? You going to tell everybody what they might be up against?"

He shook his head. "Hell no, I'm not. What good would it do? I don't figure Quanah Parker and his Comanches know June 27th from Christmas."

I said, "There were a lot of Indians down there at Hagerman's camp and they didn't even try to attack. They could have wiped us out easy. I figure that means they were waitin' for something else."

Hanrahan shrugged. He poured me another drink. "I'd appreciate it if you didn't say anything. If half the men pull out, this place is going to be pretty easy for the Comanch to overrun."

I said, "Whether you believe or not, they ought to be warned."

Hanrahan looked worried. Finally he said, "Tell you what. I'll see they're all up and wide awake before first light. That suit you?"

"How the hell you going to do that?"

"I'll do it. Don't you worry about that."

I said, "All right. I guess that's good enough."

Hanrahan looked relieved. He poured me another drink. "On the house," he said.

I finished the drink and went outside. I walked around the corral, puffing on one of the cigars, studying the fringe of timber at the meadow's edge. I could see nothing, but that didn't mean nothing was there. The horse herd, however, seemed undisturbed. They grazed placidly, halfway between the settlement and the meadow's edge.

If Indians attacked, I thought, the first thing they'd do would be to run the horses off. Yet, how could that be prevented without letting the men at the post know an attack was imminent? I guessed the Indians would just have to take the horses. If anybody brought them in and corralled them now, the men would know what was up and by dawn there wouldn't be half a dozen men left here to defend the place.

I finished my circle of the corral and stepped out into the open. I don't know what made me look back toward Hanrahan's. A sixth sense, perhaps, or maybe I sensed the murderous malice in the man standing at the rear of it.

I wasn't in time to identify the man. But I was in time to see the rifle barrel pointing at me.

It was a Sharps, and in that instant the bore looked like a cannon's bore. I flung myself forward, stumbling, but not caring, just so I moved fast. I hit the ground at the same instant the gun bellowed, and I kept going, rolling and scrambling and trying to get my own gun out in the process, so I could at least defend myself.

Once more the Sharps bellowed, and this time the slug kicked up a geyser of earth not a foot in front of my face.

It filled my eyes and right then I was totally blind and at the mercy of the man trying to murder me. Knowing it was my only chance, I got up and sprinted blindly back in what I hoped was the direction of the corral.

I hit it with enough force to stun me and bring me to my knees. Completely turned around, I didn't know from which direction the bullets had come. I had my gun in my hand, but I couldn't see to fire it.

I waited there, helplessly, for the third slug which I knew would finish me. It didn't come. I waited, my chest literally aching in the expectation of it, but it didn't come. Some men began yelling. I suppose they had just come out of Hanrahan's. I shoved my gun back into its holster and sat there knuckling the dirt out of my streaming eyes. I recognized Hanrahan's voice, not twenty feet away, and he asked, "What in the hell is going on?"

I could see him dimly now through my burning, streaming eyes. I said, "Some bastard took a couple of shots at me from behind your saloon. Damn near got me too."

"Clinger?"

"Hell, all I could see was the bore of that damn buffalo gun. It could have been Clinger. It could have been O'Malley or Westerhoff."

I got up. I was getting madder by the

minute. I said, "Let's go see where the bastards are."

Hanrahan and I walked to the saloon. He went in the front while I circled the back. There were two empty rimfire cartridges for a Sharps fifty lying on the ground, but that didn't mean anything. There must be at least two-dozen Sharps around. There were boot tracks too, the tracks of Texas high-heeled boots.

I went on around the building and went inside. Clinger was at the bar. O'Malley and Westerhoff were sitting at a table near the wall. I looked at Clinger's boots. They were Texas cowman's boots and they had high heels. O'Malley had miner's boots, but Westerhoff also had Texas boots.

I went to the table. "How long you two been here?"

O'Malley snarled, "What the hell business is that of yers?"

I said, "Tell me, ye Irish son-of-a-bitch, or I'll yank ye out of that chair and bust ye're nose fer ye." It was big talk for a man as badly beaten as I was, but when you're as mad as I was, you don't stop to think.

O'Malley started to get up, but Westerhoff pulled him back. Westerhoff said, "We been here long enough to finish most of that bottle there. That what you want to know?"

I nodded and turned away. Clinger was the only one left. He had been the one who had shot at me, but there was no use accusing him of it. Still, I was too mad to just let it go. I stepped up to the bar beside him and said, "Next time I see you with a gun in your hand, I'm going to kill you no matter whether you've shot at me or not."

√ I shouldn't have said it, because it left an opening for him to get something off his chest that he'd been wanting to get off it for a long time. He said, "Kill me and then you can have my woman. Is that it, you woman-stealin' son-of-a-bitch?"

I forgot I'd just fought him the day before yesterday. I forgot my knuckles were raw and my ribs broken and every muscle sore as a boil. I swung and caught him in the mouth and his broken stubs of teeth cut through his lips and into my knuckles like they were knives.

Hanrahan came around the end of the bar like he was shot out of a gun. He had a short club in his hand. He said angrily, "Oh no, bejesus, no more of that! Not in here at least. If you want to fight, get out where there's plenty of room. Only this time, see if one of you can't kill the other. Then maybe we'll have a little peace."

Clinger got to his feet. He came back to

139

the bar and picked up his drink. He made no move toward me and I was satisfied to let it go at that.

But I did know one thing. Before many days had passed, either Clinger or I would be dead. There could be no other way for it to end.

Chapter 13

As usual, that evening I had supper at Olds' restaurant in the rear of Rath's store. Rath was gone and so was Myers, and a few of the hunters and skinners present at the post were beginning to wonder why. There was some talk about it at the counter, but I did not participate.

Both Olds and his wife were nervous, and Mrs. Olds seemed excessively pale. Edith Clinger was plainly terrified, though of what she was afraid, I couldn't tell. It might possibly be that she was afraid of an Indian attack. More likely she was afraid of what her husband was going to do. Clinger was not in the store.

I waited until most of the other men had gone. Edith Clinger was wiping the counter in front of me. I put down my fifty cents and said, "Try not to let him catch you by surprise. Give a good loud scream, and I'll come running." I was a little surprised at myself. I had told myself repeatedly that I was going to stay out of it. Now I had to admit that my feelings had changed. The thought of Edith going back with Clinger had become intolerable to me.

She nodded. "I will. But be careful. He's capable of making me think he's taking me just to get you where he can put a bullet into you."

I said, "Don't worry about me." For an instant our eyes met, and then her glance dropped away. A flush stained her face. I could tell that she was ashamed of what had been in her eyes. She was still Clinger's wife. Thoughts such as had been apparent in her glance made her feel guilty and ashamed.

Nor was I very proud of my own thoughts. For the first time I had frankly admitted that I wanted her. Furthermore, I admitted that I would do whatever was necessary to get her.

That admission was, in itself, a bit of a shock. Was I willing to kill Clinger to get his wife? I couldn't honestly answer that question. Maybe I could kill him, but I knew I couldn't kill him in cold blood, or from ambush, or shoot him from behind. I could kill him if he tried killing me. I could kill him in the course of a fight. But not any other way.

I went outside. Tonight the breeze was coming from the west, and for once I could breathe without the everlasting stench of death cloying my nostrils. There was a good smell to the wind, of dampness as if it might rain before morning, of grass and of sagebrush and of the pungency of pinon and scrub pine on some distant hillside.

From instinct, perhaps, I stepped immediately to one side so that I would not be silhouetted against the light coming from the door. Rath's store was a soddy, so no light came through its walls. I stood there for a few moments, listening, staring into the darkness. Clinger was somewhere about, of that I was sure. I was also sure that he would kill me first chance he got. A bullet coming out of the darkness could never be traced to him. Besides that, there was no law in this place, other than the law a man made for himself.

I heard nothing and saw nothing, so I fished a cigar from my pocket. Cupping my hands to reduce the glare of the match, I lighted it. After that, whenever I took a puff I first shielded the glowing tip with a hand.

After a while, Edith Clinger came out the door. She stood for a moment in the light, wiping her hands on a towel made from a flour sack. She put up a hand and wiped the perspiration from her forehead. She said softly, "It's cool out here," as if sensing my presence and knowing I was there. It could have been the cigar, of course, but the breeze was blowing the smoke away from her rather than toward her.

I said, "It's nice to smell air that doesn't carry the stink of buffalo hides for a change."

"Yes." We stood there for several moments more, saying nothing, but, nevertheless, feeling a kind of close companionship. At last she said, "I've got to feed the Indian girl."

She went back into the store. Only moments later, I heard her cry out, and immediately after that I heard Olds shout, "Damn it, she's gone!"

I went into the store and hurried to the back. The Indian girl had been bedded down on a pile of blankets against the rear wall of the store. She must have been asleep, else she would certainly have heard the noise made cutting a hole through the sod wall of the store. The hole was big enough to admit a man, and I had to admit it could easily have been dug in less than half an hour.

Olds said, "O'Malley and Westerhoff. They're the ones that got her, sure as hell."

It was likely that they had, but it was not certain by any means. There were plenty of men in this camp who would kidnap the Indian girl just because they wanted her.

Mrs. Olds said, "Bill, you march right out there and get her back."

Olds said, "Hon, they'll blow my head off."

"Then get some help."

He looked at her, exasperated, and said, "Who the hell would help?"

Edith Clinger looked at me. She didn't say anything, but her eyes were eloquent enough. I said, "Oh hell, come on. I'll help."

I went on outside. I said, "They'll be waiting for us."

"I know it. How do you figure we ought to go about it?"

I said, "We need a diversion. Something to pull 'em away from their wagon. Or at least get one of them away."

"What do you suggest?"

I couldn't think of anything. I didn't want to fake an Indian attack because there was a good chance of a real one by sunup, and I didn't want to be responsible for making the men slow to respond to a real attack. Olds said, "We might fake a fight. Everybody knows that Clinger is itching to get at you again. If we faked a shooting, that might do the trick."

I said, "All right. Get your rifle and go over behind Myers' store. Fire two or three shots into the air, and I'll let go with a couple in return. I'll try to be close enough to O'Malley's wagon when I do. That way I can see anyone who leaves."

Olds nodded. He headed for Rath's store and I catfooted it closer to O'Malley's wagon.

I waited in the shadows of Rath's store. In the first place, I was aware that this might well be a trap aimed at both Olds and myself. Clinger might be in on it. If there was enough shooting, who could later say it was his bullet that had brought me down?

But I was committed, so I waited, and after what seemed like half an hour, but could scarcely have been more than a minute or two, a shot boomed out from behind Myers' store, then another, then another still.

Instantly a shout raised from inside Hanrahan's, but before anyone could come running out, I let go with a couple of shots of my own.

I was running before the echoes had died away, circling out toward the meadow and watching ahead of me for Olds. I saw a dim shape running and I called, "Bill? That you?"

He panted. "It's me."

Together, we headed straight for the wagon belonging to O'Malley and Westerhoff. Behind us, men came pouring out of Hanrahan's, all of them armed. Someone roared, "It's redskins! Out there! See!"

I supposed they were pointing at Olds and me because we surely were visible from the buildings, since there was a moon and it was not entirely hidden by the thin overcast. By now, though, we had reached the wagon, and now somebody howled, "They're after that goddamn Injun gal! Git 'em, boys!"

A bullet slammed into O'Malley's wagon, tearing out a chunk damn near as big as my fist. That was what a Sharps fifty could do, and I remember praying that one of them didn't hit me.

If Clinger knew I was out there, this was his golden opportunity. But right now it wasn't Clinger that scared me so much as the well-intentioned, so-called Indian fighters firing so indiscriminately.

Both of us ducked behind the wagon. The firing continued, and one more big fifty-caliber slug tore through the wagon. I looked at Olds and he looked at me. Both of us were puzzled as to the whereabouts of O'Malley and Westerhoff. If they'd been in the wagon, they'd have been out by now yelling for the shooting to stop.

I said, "I'm going in. Cover me."

He followed me to the end of the wagon. I

started to climb in, stopped suddenly when I heard a groan from inside. A cold chill ran down my spine because I knew that Indian girl might be loose in here, a knife in her hand, ready to plunge it into me.

I whispered, "O'Malley? Is that you?"

I got no answer. Just another groan. I figured I'd just as well get my feet wet, so I crawled on into the wagon. I touched something yielding, a body, and once more asked, "O'Malley?" Groping, I touched the man's face. It was not entirely cold, but neither did it have the warmth of life. This man was dead.

I went on, guided by the ragged sound of breathing. Once more encountered something yielding. It was not the Indian girl. I struck a match and saw that it was Westerhoff. His whole shirtfront was soaked with blood and he was hardly breathing at all.

I turned my head. "Yell at those damn fools to quit shooting. O'Malley's dead and Westerhoff damn near to it. The Indian girl is gone."

I crawled back out of the wagon. Olds was yelling at the men in front of the saloon to stop shooting, to bring lanterns and something to carry Westerhoff on. I got down and out of the wagon.

In a matter of minutes, the wagon was surrounded. Men with lanterns crawled inside. One yelled, "O'Malley's dead all right. Knife stickin' in his heart."

Mrs. Olds called, "How about Mr. Westerhoff?"

"Well, he's pretty damn far gone too, ma'am."

In the crowd somebody said, "If you was to ask me, I'd say both them got just what was comin' to 'em."

Mrs. Olds scolded, "That's hardly a Christian thing to say."

The same voice said, "Well ma'am, you couldn't hardly call them two Christians, no matter how much you stretched the point."

Another voice said, "I'd say we'd better, by God, find that Injun gal."

I said, "She's miles away by now."

"Then we'd better get ready for trouble, that's all I got to say. When she tells 'em what was done to her. . . ."

Olds said, "Seems to me I seen you in that line day before yestiddy."

There was nothing more from the man Olds had accused.

I walked back toward Hanrahan's. I wanted a drink. I couldn't remember having ever been this uneasy before.

From my standpoint, I ought to feel better

off. O'Malley and Westerhoff had both threatened me, and now neither one of them remained a threat. But tomorrow was the day of the predicted attack, I thought. Tomorrow was the 27th, the day Amos Chapman had said Quanah Parker and his Comanches would attack. God knew how many Indians there would be. All the Comanches Parker could muster, plus a good many hundreds of Kiowas. There would also probably be some Southern Cheyennes, since they too hunted here below the Arkansas when buffalo were scarce up north.

Hundreds of Indians against approximately thirty independent and undisciplined men. Well armed, to be sure. Good shots, all of them. But the odds weren't favorable. I suddenly wished I'd taken Edith Clinger and ridden north with Myers and Rath.

A bunch of men passed me, carrying the wounded Westerhoff. They took him into Rath's. Mrs. Olds hurried in after them. He didn't have much chance to live, but I couldn't bring myself to be sorry for him. He and O'Malley had captured that Indian girl and had treated her worse than any animal. If anybody had ever richly deserved what had happened to them, O'Malley and

Westerhoff had. I found myself hoping the Indian girl would be all right. I didn't know what Comanche custom was regarding a girl that has been raped repeatedly by the enemy. I hoped their treatment of her would be more charitable than the treatment whites would have accorded a white girl raped repeatedly by Indians.

I went into the saloon and had two drinks. Clinger was down at the end of the bar, drunk and looking quarrelsome. I didn't want any more trouble with him tonight, so I paid for my drinks and left.

I stood there in the darkness a few moments. Pretty soon Hanrahan came out, wiping sweat off his forehead with a none-too-clean apron. I said, "Tomorrow."

He knew exactly what I meant. He said, "I'm not going to bed at all tonight. I'll see to it that everyone's awake long before dawn."

Maybe he would. But I didn't intend to go to bed tonight myself. If Hanrahan didn't get them up, I would.

Because, suddenly, I was as sure as Amos Chapman had been. How they'd known the exact date, I had no idea. I was only sure that tomorrow the attack would come.

Chapter 14

The evening was little different than the others had been, except that tonight, in all the men here at Adobe Walls, there seemed to be a reluctance to go to bed. The saloon was full. Two card games were going on. A few men just paced restlessly back and forth outside.

About ten o'clock, Hanrahan came out. He said, "I'm closing up. Want a drink before I do?"

I said, "All right."

He made no move to go back inside. Instead, he looked around carefully, then said in a lowered voice, "How the hell am I going to get everybody up before dawn without looking like a goddamn old woman if the attack don't come?"

I couldn't see any way. He said, "Maybe I am an old woman. Maybe there ain't going to be no attack."

I said, "You can't be sure of that. And you don't dare take the chance."

"If I woke everybody up an' nothin' happened, I'd never live it down."

"Then tell 'em now. Tell 'em what Amos Chapman said."

"Then they'll accuse me of riskin' their necks just so's I could go on sellin' drinks. Besides that, they'll know that the Mooars and Myers and Rath ran out on them."

I turned my head and looked into the saloon. Men lined the bar, but some had already begun to spread their blankets on the floor. The ridgepole caught my glance. It must have been more than a foot thick, but it was sagging, nevertheless, from the weight of all the sod it was holding up. I said, "Fire off a pistol about three o'clock in the morning. I'll yell that the ridgepole is breaking. I guarantee that'll get 'em out of there in a hurry."

"You going to stay awake?"

"Awake and dressed."

"All right. Come on in now and have that drink."

I followed him into the saloon and he poured me a drink. I shoved a coin at him and he shoved it back. He called, "All right, boys. Finish your drinks. I'm closin' up."

I drank mine and went outside. I went to the place at the side of Myers' store where I usually slept. I sat down, holding my rifle, and put my back to the building wall.

All but one of the lights went out in

Hanrahan's. Rath's was already dark. So was Myers' store. A man came from Hanrahan's and headed toward two wagons drawn up beside Myers' corral. I recognized him as young Billy Dixon, one of the hunters who had come in from the south as a result of the Indian troubles there. He had formed a partnership with Hanrahan and had loaded up his wagons only today. He and his two skinners were planning to pull out early tomorrow to hunt north of Adobe Walls. I called, "Sleep light, Billy."

He stopped. "What is that supposed to mean?"

"Nothing. Just that there are a hell of a lot of Indians around here and I haven't heard a coyote bark all evening."

"Come to think of it, neither have I." He went on and disappeared.

Beyond Dixon's wagons were those of the Shadler brothers, Ike and Shorty. They had arrived from Dodge today with a load of supplies for Myers and Rath. They had unloaded earlier, and had then reloaded their wagons for the return trip to Dodge. They were also planning to pull out first thing tomorrow.

They tramped past, grunted at me as they passed, then made their beds on the tops of their hide wagons. A week ago I'd have marveled that they could sleep with the powerful stench of hides in their nostrils, but I knew better now. No matter where you slept here at Adobe Walls, the stench was overpowering. And it was barely possible that, on top of the piled-up hides, the breeze blew the stench away. I thought about warning them the way I had Billy Dixon, then decided against it. Both Ike and Shorty were old-timers and they were always on their guard.

I lighted a cigar. The last lamp inside Hanrahan's went out. I saw a dim figure come from the doorway of the saloon. It was Hanrahan coming toward me. He sat down and put his back against the wall of Myers' store.

I asked, "How come you're going into partnership with Billy Dixon if you think there's going to be an Indian attack?"

He said, "Hell, you can't stop doin' everything just because you think somethin's going to happen, can you?"

I said, "Guess not. Seen Clinger anywhere?"

"Uh uh. He wasn't in the saloon, an' he sure as hell wouldn't be sleepin' over at Rath's."

I was leaning against the outside wall of Myers' store. It was built of small logs set upright in a trench which had been dug in the ground for that purpose. They were set as close as possible, but there still were cracks between each pole, some wide enough to shove a gun barrel through, some only wide enough for the blade of a knife. I said, "I think I'll settle down over there by the corral."

Hanrahan laughed. "Just occur to you that Clinger might be inside Myers' place?"

"Well, he could be."

Hanrahan said, "I saw him go in O'Keefe's smithy a while ago. I expect that's where he is."

I picked up my rifle and other gear. "Just the same, I think I'll feel better over by the corral."

He got up and came with me. We settled down with our backs to the corral, in a spot where we could see the horse herd and all the buildings as well. If we peered through the corral, we could see Billy Dixon's wagons and those of the Shadler brothers a little farther out.

O'Malley's wagon stood empty where they had left it near the stream. I listened for night sounds, but I couldn't hear any. No coyote barked. No owl hooted. I did hear the distant howl of a wolf, and an answering one, but both must have been over half a mile away. I said, "I wonder if they're out there. And if they are, I wonder how many of 'em."

Hanrahan said, "Well, if they're out there, they's a hell of a lot of 'em. It's supposed to be Quanah Parker headin' 'em, an' he wouldn't come unless he had four or five hundred bucks."

Quanah Parker was the son of Cynthia Ann Parker, who had been kidnapped as a child by the Comanches. She'd grown up with the tribe, married a Comanche, and had ultimately borne a son who had become one of the most bloodthirsty of all Comanche chiefs. Despite his half-white heritage, he hated whites more than a Baptist preacher hates sin.

I said, "You should have brought a jug."

Hanrahan chuckled. "Don't think I didn't think of it. I changed my mind. Figured you and me needed clear heads when morning came."

We sat in silence for a time after that. Then Hanrahan asked, "What brought you up here? Huntin' buffalo ain't exactly the kind of thing a man chooses all by hisself."

I said, "Money. I been working for somebody else all my life. I figured, after one summer of hunting buffalo, I could make enough to get me started on a place of my own."

He said, "That Clinger's wife is a damn good woman."

I asked, "What is that supposed to mean?"

"Well, she says she's leavin' him. An' you sure as hell could do worse."

I said, "I'm not gettin' mixed up between a husband and his wife."

Hanrahan laughed. "Ain't you the holy one? You think you ain't mixed up?"

"Well, it wasn't my doing. I couldn't leave her to walk all the way to Dodge, could I?"

"No, an' you couldn't help fightin' her old man either, could you?"

Hanrahan was a likable man and I knew he was joshing me. I said, "Ah shut up."

He said, "Clinger ain't going to forget the beating you gave him. He's a goddamn bully, an' bullies don't take to gettin' beat."

"I didn't figure he'd forget."

"He ain't going to let you leave this place alive. Especially if you try takin' his wife to Dodge."

"Maybe the Indians will beat him to my scalp."

I changed the subject then. I asked, "What are you doin' away down here? Saloon business better here than it is in Dodge?"

"It sure as hell is, especially if you got the only saloon for two hundred miles. Man can get three times what a drink brings in Dodge, an' freightin' the stuff in here ain't all that expensive, bein' as there's wagons comin' down here empty anyways. I figure by the end of the summer I can build me the biggest an' fanciest saloon in Dodge."

I didn't mention the possibility that the Indian attack tomorrow, if it came, would change his plans. I said, "Want to sleep a while? I'll stay awake."

"All right." He settled himself more comfortably and within ten minutes was snoring lustily.

I got up. My revolver was in its holster, fully loaded. I picked up the new Sharps I'd bought and loaded it. The pockets of my coat were sagging with extra cartridges. I didn't intend to be caught short if I could help it.

The silence was eerie. There was no cry from a night bird, no sound of any kind. I stared at O'Keefe's smithy, where Hanrahan had said Clinger was bedded down. I walked around the corral and out into the meadow. My horse raised his head but he didn't look at me. He looked in the opposite direction, ears pricked forward, as if he had seen something.

I pulled the picket pin and coiled the rope.

I'd intended to move him, but I changed my mind. I led him in and put him into the corral along with the half dozen or so others that were there.

I was nervous, so I walked down to the creek and got a drink. O'Malley's wagon stood empty and gaunt against the cloudy, moon-brightened sky. I couldn't feel sorry for the way O'Malley had died. I couldn't pity Westerhoff.

I walked back. Hanrahan must have heard me because he sat bolt upright. "What time is it?"

"Two-thirty, I suppose. It's too dark to see a watch."

"Light a match and look."

I stepped behind him, putting him between O'Keefe's smithy and me. I struck a match, opened the hunting case of my big silver watch, and looked at it. It was two-twenty. Hanrahan said, "It's time."

I said, "Wait until I get over in front of the saloon."

"Go ahead." I walked to the saloon. I was immediately in front of the door when Hanrahan fired his pistol into the air.

In spite of the fact that I was expecting it, I jumped. I howled, "Christ, boys, the ridge-pole's breakin'! Get the hell out before it buries us!"

I stood aside as they came pouring out of the saloon. Most of them were carrying their clothes and boots. Most also had their guns. Down here in Indian country a man never went anywhere without his gun, not even to the outhouse.

Hanrahan came running now, and apparently nobody noticed that both Hanrahan and I were fully dressed. Hanrahan said, "For God's sake, boys, find a pole to prop the son-of-a-bitch up! If that roof comes down nobody will get a drink for a whole goddamn week."

The men dressed hastily, strapped on their guns, leaned their rifles against the sod wall of the saloon, and scattered to try and find a pole long enough and strong enough to prop up the ridgepole of the saloon. From Rath's, somebody inquired what all the damn racket was about. Several lanterns were lighted. Carrying one of them, a man went into the saloon. He held the lantern high, peering at the ridgepole and looking for a crack. He said, "Hell, I can't see a thing."

Hanrahan yelled, "Find a pole and fix it, boys, and the drinks are on the house."

More men scattered because free drinks for everyone were not everyday happenings. Men carried half a dozen poles to the saloon, took them in, and raised them to see if they would fit. The fifth one was long enough, and everybody thought it was strong enough. Somebody found a saw and a man shinnied up the pole to mark the place where it should be cut.

Ten minutes later it was in place, securely jammed against the middle of the ridgepole which was, in reality, just as strong as the day it had been put up. All the men now streamed into the saloon. From the doorway, Hanrahan bawled in the general direction of Rath's, "Drinks are on the house, boys, for everyone. Come and get 'em. All you can drink, by God!"

That, in itself, should have been enough to raise the men's suspicions. Hanrahan simply wasn't that generous.

But nobody seemed to question it. They streamed into the saloon and lined the bar, and for a while Hanrahan had all he could do filling their tin cups for them.

Chapter 15

For an hour everyone whooped it up in Hanrahan's saloon, drinking more than they ordinarily would because the drinks were free. I began to worry that the whole damn kit and caboodle would be too drunk to fight if and when the Indians attacked. The same thing was obviously worrying Hanrahan, but he didn't dare stop giving out free drinks. The minute he did, all the men would have staggered back to bed.

A fight started between two men, and a ring formed. Although both were too drunk to hit each other with any force, it did pass almost twenty minutes. I went to the door. It was nearly four and the eastern sky was beginning to show the faintest tinge of gray.

A few men even now began drifting back to their beds. Hanrahan yelled, "Hell, boys, it's purty near daylight now. No use going back to bed. I'll bet Bill Olds an' his wife will have coffee goin' afore long."

Nobody seemed to pay much attention to him. Hanrahan called out to Billy Dixon, "Billy, go out an' run in the horses. Get Billy

Ogg an' Jess Burdett here to give you a hand. Long as you're up, you'd just as well get an early start for the hunting grounds."

Dixon rolled up his bed and went out the door, his Sharps in his other hand. I followed, and Billy Ogg came after me. I understood Hanrahan's strategy. He thought maybe the three of us could get the horses corralled before the attack.

Billy Dixon said, "I'll go toss my bedroll up on the wagon. You and Ogg get hosses out of the corral an' drive the bunch in. I'll open the gate."

I got my saddle from the top corral pole and carried it to the gate. My horse was still inside the corral where I'd put him last night. I roped him and put the bridle on. I was about to throw the saddle up when I heard Billy Dixon shout.

He was over beside his wagon and had just thrown his bedroll up. He bawled, "Too late for the hosses, boys. Look at them sons-a-bitches come!"

I threw my saddle back onto the top corral pole and ran for my Sharps, leaning against the poles. Dixon bawled, "Watch me get a couple of 'em when they try to run the hosses off."

He shot once, the deep-throated roar of the Sharps shocking in the morning silence.

I don't know whether he hit anything or not because immediately I heard him shout, "By God, boys, they ain't after the hosses! They're comin' straight at us."

I was already outside the corral. Billy Ogg, who had headed out into the meadow afoot, came running back as fast as he could go. I headed for Hanrahan's saloon, out of whose doorway men were now streaming to take a look. From O'Keefe's smithy Clinger ran, wearing nothing but his red, long-handled underwear. Olds and his wife and Edith Clinger came from Rath's, along with several others who had apparently been sleeping there.

At the doorway of Hanrahan's, I stopped and turned to look. I swear to God, I have never seen that many Indians all together in my whole damn life. There must have been four or five hundred of them, galloping their horses full tilt toward us in a long, wavering line. Feathered headdresses and horses' manes bannered out in the wind, and most of the Indians waved rifles, not shooting yet because they weren't close enough. A group broke away from the main bunch and drove the horses off. In minutes the horses and their Indian drovers disappeared over a hill.

Well, I'd known that the horses were the first things the Indians would go for if they ever did attack, and I had not been wrong. I was glad I had my horse inside the corral, although what good he'd do me, I didn't know. There wasn't going to be any getting through the number of Indians that had this place surrounded, unless maybe a man could do it in the dead of night when the Indians were off their guard.

I was already anticipating a long siege. Why I didn't assume that all those Indians would just wipe us out, was based on white man's arrogance, I suppose. Like Fetterman, maybe I thought eighty good troopers could ride through the whole damn bunch of them.

They were close in now, and beginning to shoot even though they weren't hitting anything. Everybody crowded into the saloon, and a minute later Billy Ogg arrived panting from his long sprint across the meadow. He fell on the dirt floor of the saloon, breathing hard, soaked with sweat, and trembling.

O'Keefe, who was in the saloon, ran out suddenly. He headed toward Rath's to rouse anybody still asleep, saw Olds in the doorway, and then turned and ran for Myers' store to rouse those still asleep in there. From the saloon doorway, I looked past the corral toward the Indians and saw Ike and Shorty Shadler raising up sleepily, roused by the yelps and shots.

They were engulfed by the first wave of Indians. Their wagon was surrounded. They died almost instantly, each shot half a dozen times and pierced with arrows too. Both fell from the high wagon to the ground, and were immediately surrounded by Indians, who had dismounted to take their scalps.

I opened fire with my Sharps, knowing as I did so that I couldn't stop the scalping and that it didn't matter anyway. Ike and Shorty were both dead. Their big dog, who had been sleeping under the wagon, ran out growling and snarling and attacked the Indians surrounding his two masters. He was shot with half a dozen bullets and his throat cut as a final savage gesture.

I ducked back into the saloon and looked around. Dixon and Ogg were here, along with a man named Masterson, who was nicknamed Bat. Others here were Oscar Sheppard, Mike Welch, Hiram Watson, Jim McKinley, and Bermuda Carlisle. Hanrahan was here, of course, and so was Argo. He was standing in the doorway, staring out toward the wagon where DeValois was bedded down. He muttered, "The goddamn Injuns will get him. The son-of-a-bitch ain't goin' to hang if I let the Indians get hold of him."

He started out, but I grabbed his arm. I said, "No use you gettin' killed. Gettin' caught by them Indians is a heap worse than gettin' hanged."

It was a cold-blooded thing to say, but I knew Argo hadn't a chance of making it out to that wagon, getting DeValois out, and dragging him back here without getting killed himself.

The Indians reached the wagon where DeValois was and a couple of them looked inside. They whooped with glee and a dozen of them piled off their horses and crawled up on the wagon.

They dragged DeValois out. He was already hurt pretty bad, and the rough handling they gave him must have caused him a lot of pain. But his screaming wasn't as much from pain as from sheer terror because he knew exactly what they were going to do to him, and he knew how long it would probably take him to die. I guess I ought to have felt sorry for any man facing what DeValois faced, but I somehow couldn't feel very sorry for him. I turned my head and looked at Argo's face. His eyes were gleaming and his jawline was hard with knotted muscles. He said, "It's goin' to be harder than hangin' all right, the dirty son-of-a-bitch! By God, I hope they make him last long enough to go through somethin' of what he put my little girl through!"

I said, "They will. They're experts at making a man last. Likely won't even lose consciousness."

There was a lot of shooting from between the upright poles of Myers' store and O'Keefe's and from the doorway of Hanrahan's.

There weren't any real portholes to shoot through, and it's pretty damn hard to hit anything when you're shooting through a crack that's barely big enough to stick the barrel of your gun through, so I can't say we did those redskins much harm during their first charge. I never did see what was done with DeValois. The charge itself overran the ones who had dragged him out of his wagon. They crossed the open space between, so fast, it took a man's breath away. I ducked back into Hanrahan's. The thunder of the Indian horses' hoofs drowned out almost everything but the gunshots and the triumphant howls of the Indians. They came right up to the door of Hanrahan's and I shot one just as he pulled his horse to a plunging halt.

The buck came somersaulting over his horse's head, hit the ground just in front of the door, and rolled on in. He knocked one man down and staggered another, but he was stone dead before he ever hit the ground.

Hanrahan bawled, "Get out there an' give 'em a fight, boys, or by God they're goin' to take this place!"

He was right too. There must have been two hundred Indians within fifty feet of the buildings, their horses millin', shooting at anything that moved. Hagerman was the first to charge out through the door. Instantly, he ducked to one side of it to get out of the way of those coming behind.

He had a Sharps in each hand. I followed him out, and for a few minutes I was too busy shooting to worry about Hagerman. But I could hear the regularly spaced roar of his Sharps, and every time one of those big guns roared, either an Indian or an Indian horse went down. Mostly he hit the Comanches themselves, but once in a while a horse's head would get in the way and catch the slug meant for his rider.

I glanced aside, my fingers cramming in a rimfire cartridge by feel, and shaking so badly it was pretty hard to do.

It was like Hagerman was on a buffalo stand, I thought, because he was down on his rump, elbows resting on his spraddled knees to steady the aim of his big buffalo gun. He didn't even seem aware of the bullets thudding into the sod walls of Hanrahan's saloon, and I know he didn't hear the sound of any gun but his own.

His face was shiny with sweat and grimed and black with powder, but the look in his eyes was crazy, something like the look I'd seen in Argo's eyes when the Indians took DeValois.

Even as I shot him that short glance, my shaking fingers closed the action of my gun. Before I could look away I saw him take an arrow in the shoulder. It must have gone in a couple of inches at least and it quivered as it slammed his shoulder back against the sod wall. If anything, I thought his eyes gleamed more fiercely and savagely, as if pain had somehow given him more strength and more resolve than he'd had before.

I didn't dare look at him any longer, though. I had my own troubles. An Indian nearly as big as I am but a lot shorter and bandy-legged, left his horse and came at me with a knife. I shot him in the chest and it didn't stop him or hardly slow him down. As I jumped to one side, his knife buried itself to the hilt in the sod wall of the saloon.

My gun was empty and there wasn't any time to reload. He was turning, his chest a welter of blood from an artery pumping it out through the big hole made by my

Sharps. I clubbed the gun and brought its barrel down as hard as I could right on the top of his head.

The sound was solid. The kind of sound you don't forget if you live to be a hundred. It crushed his skull and made a dent the shape of the rifle barrel in the top of his head. It must have been an inch deep at least.

Well, the bullet hadn't stopped him, but that blow with the heavy barrel of my Sharps did. Or maybe it just finished the bullet's work. That Indian should have been dead twice over, but he wasn't even dead when he hit the ground at my feet. He was unconscious and he couldn't fight any more, but his chest was still going up and down, and the blood was still pumping in red spurts out of the hole I'd put there.

But there wasn't time to worry about him. I heard Hanrahan bawl, "They're pulling back! For God's sake, boys, get under cover!"

A lot of the men ducked inside the saloon. A couple stayed in the doorway, still shooting regularly. One of these was Masterson, the other, Argo, the bounty hunter. I decided I'd been enough of a hero for one day. I made for the saloon doorway too, nearly knocking Masterson down as I went through.

From inside, I looked back out. The wagon where DeValois had been was burning from a torch thrown into it. There was no sign of DeValois, nor of the Indians who had captured him. They'd hauled him away to torture him, undisturbed, I guessed.

The wave of Indians galloped away, but not quite out of rifle range. They milled around out there, apparently arguing among themselves and trying to decide what they ought to do. Two or three took cover down in the bed of the little creek and began sniping with deadly accuracy at the defenders who were still exposed. I heard a yell from the right side of the door, and heard Masterson shout, "Come on in, Hagerman, before they kill you! You won't kill any more damn Comanch if you're dead yourself!"

I suppose it was that argument that helped Hagerman decide to come inside. Carrying his two smoking-hot Sharps, he came stumbling into the doorway. He staggered across the room to the bar and put his two guns on it. He reached for a bottle and took a drink out of it like it was water. He glanced at me and said harshly, "Get this goddamn thing out of me."

I went over to him and I could see blood

on the back of his shirt, so I knew the arrow had gone through. By this time the Comanches were getting metal arrowheads from the white man, so to leave one in was as deadly as leaving a bullet in. I said, "I'll have to push it on through enough to grab the point. Then I'll have to break it off and pull it through."

He said, "Do it," and took another drink. I said, "Put that bottle down and hold onto the bar."

He did. I grabbed the arrow shaft and pushed. His face turned white and twisted with the pain, but he didn't make a sound. I tried breaking the arrow without hurting him any more, but it was impossible. When it was broken, I grabbed the iron arrowhead and pulled it through.

He was still conscious, but he was white and barely able to hold himself upright. I asked, "Where'd the bullet hit?"

"Leg. Went on through."

I said, "I'll pour some whiskey on your shoulder. You put some on your leg." I took the bottle and soaked the arrow wound, front and back. He dumped some on his leg, then dumped some more down his throat. He reached for his Sharps.

I said, "Rest a minute, for God's sake. The Indians will keep."

He growled, "Like hell they will," and staggered toward the door. He pushed Argo aside, rested the barrel of his Sharps on the doorjamb, and began firing.

Chapter 16

Here in this isolated outpost nobody was in charge, and nobody seemed willing to take charge. Myers was gone, and so was Rath and so were the Mooars brothers, any one of whom might have been capable of guiding the failing destinies of the handful of whites pitted against so many well-armed Indians. The first charge had come as an almost complete surprise. Had the whites been asleep as the Indians expected, they would have been wiped out to a man. They had not been asleep because of Amos Chapman's warning, and because Hanrahan had believed in it sufficiently to wake the men with a cock-and-bull story about a cracked ridgepole in the saloon.

I was a Johnny-come-lately and had no intention of taking charge, besides which, I doubted if anyone would have accepted me. Hagerman was a madman, intent only on killing Indians. Argo's thirst for vengeance was satisfied. DeValois was dead or soon to die at the Comanches' hands, and Argo seemed almost disinterested in what was happening.

It was up to Hanrahan. He was not a born leader, but he was one of the founders of this post. I looked at him while the Indians, about a quarter mile away, milled around uncertainly, and I said, "You'd better, by God, take hold or they'll wipe us out next time. There ain't enough men can shoot from that doorway to do any good."

For an instant he looked scared of the responsibility, but he was a good man and it didn't take him long to get his thinking straightened out. He bawled, "There's grain sacks and flour sacks in both Rath's and Myers' stores! Get your asses over there and throw up some breastworks in front that a man can shoot over!"

Well, this was what I wanted, to get over to Rath's where Edith was and be with her to personally make damn sure that nothing happened to her. I knew what happened to women when the Indians got hold of them, particularly Comanches and the other plains tribes. I ran out of the saloon door, bending low and carrying my new Sharps. There were cartridges aplenty in Rath's, and I was getting low.

Rath's store was, like the saloon, built of sod, so it wasn't too likely that anyone inside of it had yet been hit by Comanche bullets, which had been flying around thick and fast but were not too carefully aimed. The store was straight south of Hanrahan's. I made a beeline for it, running as fast as I could and bending low.

I guess I should have thought about O'Keefe's smithy being behind me, and I should have remembered Clinger running out of it earlier in his red flannel underwear. He'd sure as hell be going back for the rest of his clothes. I didn't think, however. I was too concerned with the six or seven hundred Indians milling around out there just getting up their courage for another charge which, if we weren't more ready than we'd been the first time, would sweep over us and wipe us out in less time than it takes to tell about it.

Anyhow, something hit me in the leg and it felt like the kick of a mule. My leg collapsed under me and I went skidding along the ground on my face for a couple of feet before I began to roll. There wasn't much shooting going on right then. It was fairly easy to pick out the roar of a rifle coming from the cracks between the upright stakes of O'Keefe's smithy and to guess who the hell they were coming from. Clinger had said he'd kill me first chance he got, and it looked like this was his chance. A second bullet tore up a shower of dirt not six inches from my head, and a third took the heel off my right boot as clean as if it had been done with an axe.

Rath's doorway was still twenty-five feet ahead of me and I didn't see how the hell I was going to make it with Clinger shooting at me while I tried. There was only one thing to do and that was fight back. My leg was numb and I knew I was hurt bad. If Clinger's bullet had cut an artery, I didn't have much chance, since there wasn't a doctor closer than Dodge, close to a hundred miles away.

I scooted around like some kind of crab, I guess, until I had my face toward O'Keefe's, and as I did, Clinger fired again. This time the bullet sprayed dirt into my face, but some lucky reflex had made me close my eyes so that they weren't filled with it. I opened them, knowing, from the bluish powder smoke drifting away from it, exactly what part of O'Keefe's the shot had come from. I shoved my gun out in front of me, took a bead on that spot, and let fly. Before I even took notice of where the bullet hit, I was fumbling in my coat for another cartridge and shoving it into the breach.

Splinters flew from the place on O'Keefe's smithy. That big, fifty-caliber slug damn near cut one of the upright poles in two.

Soon as I got loaded, I let fly again at the same spot, and then while I fumbled for yet another cartridge, I got up and ran for Rath's, zigzagging back and forth trying to throw off Clinger's aim. I'd made him draw back, even if I hadn't hit him, and had scared him enough to make him more careful next time he took a shot at me. I figured I might, if I was lucky, have enough time to get in the door at Rath's.

Well, I did, and nobody was more surprised than me. I slammed into somebody, knocking him down and falling almost on top of him, and the body I hit was soft, not like that of a man, but like a woman's. Soon as I got my wits about me, I looked to see who it was. It was Edith Clinger. I was lying half on top of her, and I pushed away real quick. I know my face was red and I felt hot, and all of it wasn't from the sprint between Hanrahan's and here. I said, "Ma'am, I'm sorry. I sure hope I didn't hurt you none." All I could think about was how soft the parts of her I'd touched had been. Even in that minute after being shot at by her husband and wondering if the Comanches were going to wipe us out, I caught myself wondering what it would be like to go to bed with her.

Her face was just as red as mine, and we got to our feet and stood there staring at each other for a couple of seconds. Then I remembered what I was supposed to do and I yelled, "Get all the grain sacks and flour sacks you can find and carry 'em outside. We got to throw up some kind of breastworks, so that the next time them damn Indians charge we'll have enough rifles workin' to drive 'em back!"

Well, everybody got busy, and the two women did what women always do in times of stress. They went back there and got the stove going and they put on food to feed the fighting men.

I carried out a hundred-pound sack of grain and went back for another one, and another one after that. I carried out five before the Indians regrouped and came charging in again. I made one more running trip into Rath's for rimfire cartridges for my Sharps fifty, and then I went out and threw myself down behind the sacks.

Looking toward the Indians, I could now see one who seemed to be giving the others hell. He was naked as a jaybird, except for a coat of bright yellow paint all over him. Now Indians have all kinds of medicine and superstitions, and this was his, I guessed. He figured that yellow paint was magic and wouldn't let any of the white man's bullets hit him.

I didn't know any of the Indians by name, except for Quanah Parker, and I wouldn't have known him if I'd stood face to face with him. But I learned later that the yellow Indian was Isatai, a young Comanche medicine man, and although he wasn't a chief, he was surely acting like one.

The haranguing went on for five or ten more minutes, minutes we sure as hell needed. Men kept coming out of both Rath's and Myers' stores carrying sacks. They piled them up along the front walks of the store. They brought out ammunition too, enough of it to fight Indians for a week. That was sure one advantage these men had being down here hunting buffalo. They had all the supplies they needed, guns and ammunition enough to wipe out a hundred thousand buffalo.

Now that I was down behind the breastworks, I had time to look at my leg. I'd been able to walk and carry grain sacks, so I knew no bone was broken. It was bleeding quite a lot, but the blood came steady and not in spurts, and it was darker than blood that comes from a severed artery.

I took my knife and slit my pants up as high as the bullet hole. The one going in was about the size of a dime, and just oozing blood, but the one in back was a couple of inches across, and shredded from the expanding bullet Clinger had used on me. Most of the blood was coming from where the bullet had come out.

Billy Dixon was there beside me and he said, "Hold still. I'll get you some whiskey and bandages from the saloon."

Before I could say anything, he was up and gone. In a minute he was back. He handed me a brown bottle of whiskey, then dashed into Rath's, probably to ask one of the women for part of her petticoat. I took a stiff drink out of the bottle because the leg was beginning to hurt like hell, and poured some over the wound. That hurt so bad I almost let go of the bottle. My head began to whirl and I only half realized that Billy Dixon was back and that Edith Clinger was along with him.

I did have enough strength and sense to look toward the smithy and I told Dixon, "Throw some sacks up between me and O'Keefe's. That's where the bullet came from."

Edith was down on her knees. She had compresses and strips of cloth in her hands. She soaked a compress with whiskey and laid it on the exit wound. She watched my face, seeing how it hurt, and to take my mind off the pain she asked, "Was it my husband that shot you, Mr. Burdett?"

I said, "I figure. He's the only one with reason, now that O'Malley's dead and Westerhoff's laid up."

She didn't say any more, but busied herself binding up my leg. Now that there were breastworks in front of both the sod buildings, Rath's and Hanrahan's, men began carrying sacks to the two stake buildings. These they placed inside in order to create some kind of protection for the men.

Suddenly a big yell went up out there in the meadow where the Indians were. And after that there was a lot of thunder in the ground, seeming to shake it the way a dynamite explosion might. It was the thunder of thousands of horses' hoofs, pounding straight toward us and growing louder with every second that fled past.

My leg was hurting, but Edith Clinger was through with it now and I pushed her toward the doorway of Rath's and said, "You get inside. Hurry up! There's nothing more you can do for me."

She didn't hesitate. She ran for the door and disappeared inside. I was light-headed from the whiskey I'd drunk, and I was probably dizzy from the pain of my wound. Besides that, the range was still too far for accurate shooting, although some of the boys had already begun to shoot.

So I took time to look, knowing in my heart that this was something I would never see again. Maybe it was something no man would.

The line of Indian warriors must have been nearly a quarter mile long, and behind them was another line almost as long, being held in reserve.

All of them were painted, in varying degrees, from the naked Isatai painted entirely yellow from head to foot, to the ones who had only a few streaks of paint on their faces and on their naked chests.

There were the headdresses of the chiefs, and the feathers of the braves, each of which signified a coup counted upon an enemy. Feathers and plumes fluttered from lances, and most of the horses had some kind of fluttering decoration in their manes. They yelled like maniacs, and even I, inexperienced with Indian warfare, knew the reason for all this. The Rebels had yelled thus during the Civil War, the reason being to demoralize the enemy.

Most times it worked, too, but not today. Not with this small, outnumbered group of whites. Each of them was experienced in fighting Indians. Each was a marksman, a man used to great odds, used to depending on himself. They didn't need a commander now. They didn't need anyone to tell them when to shoot.

The wave of Indians crossed the creek and came on, splitting around O'Malley's abandoned wagon. And now the men behind the breastworks began firing.

Boom! Boom! Boom! No small guns here. All were big ones, meant for buffalo, and most of them were Sharps fifties like the one I had. You had to reload after every shot, but it didn't take very long, and most of the men had a pile of rimfire cartridges on the ground beside them. They were so experienced, they could pick them up by feel without ever taking their eyes off the Indians.

I got a bead on an Indian who was short and squat and middle-aged. I squeezed off the trigger the way I'd have done if he'd been a deer, or the way I'd done during the war. It looked like he'd run into a rope stretched between two trees. He was driven back off his horse's rump and he hit the ground on his back. The forward motion of his body made him roll, but he was already dead. When his body came to rest it lay still, spread-eagled, with sightless eyes staring up at the sky.

Might be it was silly, but I felt guilty for

having killed that Indian. I told myself he'd have killed me if he could, but it didn't help. Because killing him was wrong. We had no business being here, and no right to do what we were here to do. We were spoilers, wasters, killing animals that meant life to the plains Indians and leaving their carcasses to rot while we took only the hide. It didn't matter that I hadn't killed any buffalo yet. I'd come here to kill them and that made me just as guilty as everybody else.

But guilty or not, a man tries to stay alive, and I went on shooting. I hit another Indian, and killed a third one's horse before they got a belly full of our accurate fire and galloped back out of range again, howling with the bitterness of frustration and defeat.

I sank back and closed my eyes. For a moment I was very weak and sick, and I hurt so much, I didn't care what happened next.

Chapter 17

Dimly I heard Billy Dixon say, "They're gone for now. And if you ask me we'd better do somethin' about that son-of-a-bitch over there in O'Keefe's that keeps shootin' at Burdett. I don't mind him shootin' at Burdett, but we're all here close together, and Clinger's just as likely to get one of us as he is Burdett."

I forced myself up to a sitting position. I said, "You keep your goddamn noses out of my business. I'll take care of him."

"Sure. Like you just did when he cut that leg out from under you. Besides, if you kill him you ain't goin' to have a chance with that woman of his."

He said it in a perfectly matter-of-fact way. He wasn't making any insinuations and he wasn't trying to insult anybody. I figured it would be pretty small of me to take offense. Still, I couldn't let other men risk their lives messing in trouble that was strictly mine.

I'd been shot in the leg, and while I'd even lugged sacks for breastworks after I got the wound, I'd done so before the shock wore off and the pain set in. The leg hurt now like bloody hell, but no worse than a belly wound I'd gotten during the war and I'd kept going then. Besides, my leg had been bandaged and I didn't need to worry either about too much bleeding or getting dirt in it.

I pushed myself up and, using the Sharps fifty as a support, headed for O'Keefe's. Almost instantly a puff of smoke blossomed from between two of the stoutest poles.

At the same time, or maybe just before, Billy Dixon stuck out his foot and I tripped on it. I fell forward and I guess that's all that saved my life. Only I wasn't thinking just then that it had saved my life. The fall made knives of pain shoot all the way to my shoulders. It made bright spots dance before my eyes and made me so dizzy and weak I didn't know if I'd ever get up again.

Only pure fury made it possible for me to push myself to my knees. I glared at Billy Dixon and I said, "You dirty son-of-a-bitch!"

Dixon grinned. "Sure. Now you lay still before I have to clout you on the head."

He turned his head and said, "Who's going with me to get that bushwhackin' bastard!"

I wasn't seeing very well, but there wasn't anything wrong with my hearing. Half a dozen men said they'd go and maybe they were doing it so they wouldn't be exposed to bullets aimed at me. Maybe they weren't, too. I put forth more effort than I ever have before or since in my life. I managed to push myself up to my feet both by using my rifle as a support and by clawing at a man standing next to me. I said, "You ain't going without me, by God!"

Dixon said, "This is for your own good, Burdett," and slugged me on the point of the chin.

Well, a feather would've knocked me over and Dixon's bony fist wasn't any feather. I fell and lit on my back and everything went black.

Dixon hadn't hit any harder than he had to, so I couldn't have been out very long. When I came to, I could hear somebody yelling about them having no right to do this to him. They couldn't prove he'd done anything, and anyhow they wasn't lawmen and they'd better let him loose. It was Clinger's voice and, from the sound of it, I guess he thought they were going to string him up.

I clawed at the grain sacks enough to see over them. Dixon and some others had got hold of Clinger and were dragging him toward Hanrahan's, probably to tie him up until this Indian attack was over with.

All of a sudden I heard the damnedest sound I'd heard since I got mustered out of the army after the war. It was the brassy notes of an Army bugle blowing the "Charge."

I jerked my head around and saw the Indians coming in again, just about the same as they had the first time, a long line leading, and a shorter, second line hanging back in reserve.

I guess there's no reason why an Indian can't learn to blow a bugle the same as a white man can, and there's always a lot of so-called "friendlies" hanging around every Army post. They're not always so damned friendly, and a good part of the time they're hostiles hanging around to see what they can find out about patrols and escort movements and the post's manpower and capabilities. But, hanging around like that, it'd be easy enough for an Indian who already knew how to blow the bugle to learn the various Army calls. For coordinating things during action, a bugle beats yelling, any day.

Between me and O'Keefe's smithy, Dixon and the others stopped like they'd been frozen. I suppose they thought the U.S. cavalry was galloping to our rescue, but it didn't take them long to see their mistake. They saw that damned Indian and they saw the sun glint on his brass bugle and they heard again the stirring notes of the charge.

The line of Indians wasn't any less impressive this time than it had been before. Dixon and the others forgot all about Clinger. The Indians were almost to the creek already and that was inside the range of an Indian's gun. Dixon and the others let go of Clinger and streaked toward the breastworks where I was because that was where all their guns and ammunition were.

Uncertain, Clinger stood out there for a long moment. I could tell he was trying to decide what he ought to do, but he sure didn't have much time. He was unarmed, Dixon and the others having forced him to leave his gun behind at O'Keefe's. If he went back to O'Keefe's, he knew that some of the men holed up there might make him a prisoner and hold him for Dixon to come get after the Indians had been repulsed.

He hesitated just a little bit too long. The Indians were almost to him when he finally made up his mind. He sprinted for Myers' store, running faster than I'd have believed a man his size could run.

He almost made it, too. Beside me, Dixon and the others were concentrating their fire on the Indians closest to Clinger and two of them went down, but it didn't save Clinger. A squat, heavyset buck, naked to the waist and painted red and yellow and black, leaned far to the right as his horse galloped past, and clouted Clinger right on top of the head with his stone tomahawk.

There was a lot of noise, Indians yelling, horses' hoofs pounding, guns going off, but even in the midst of all that noise I heard the sound the tomahawk made striking Clinger's skull. I heard the scream, too, that must have come from Edith Clinger's throat as she saw Clinger fall.

Another Indian, a young one, leaped off his horse, knife in hand, and headed for Clinger to take his scalp. Billy Dixon sighted coolly, as if he was shooting buffalo, and dropped that young buck while he was still half a dozen yards away from where Clinger lay. There might have been some others with ideas of taking Clinger's scalp or counting coup on him, but when they saw that young brave go down, they lost interest quickly. The charge swept between the buildings and beyond, and split to right and left, and before we knew it, the reserve line was right on top of us.

In the first charge, a horse had been shot out from under an Indian who was dressed up like a chief. He was still on foot out there, and suddenly I heard someone yell from the direction of Myers' store. "That's Parker! That's Quanah Parker! Kill the son-of-a-bitch!"

Bullets began kicking up dust all around the chief, if that was really who he was, but he wouldn't run. He just stood there, as if he had some medicine that would keep the bullets from touching him. Another brave swept by and leaned over and gave the chief a hand. Quanah Parker swung up behind him while the horse was still in mid-gallop. Horse and both riders disappeared behind O'Keefe's smithy, with neither rider nor the horse even grazed, in spite of all the lead that had been thrown at them.

It was uncanny, and maybe it was right that Quanah Parker had some kind of medicine that kept bullets from hitting him. I felt a chill run along my spine at the thought, and then I cursed myself disgustedly under my breath. I was weak and dizzy and probably a little delirious or I wouldn't be thinking such silly thoughts.

The line of reserves went through the buildings and split the same as the first line had, and for several minutes all was quiet. There was no firing, and when anybody said anything it was in a shout, as if he needed to make himself heard over the noise, only there wasn't any noise. Every time he'd look sheepish and lower his voice. Masterson said, "Billy, do you think Clinger's still alive? If he is, I'll go out there an' drag him in."

Dixon said, "Hell no, he ain't alive. I could hear the sound of that tomahawk hittin' him away over here, even with all the other noise there was. Leave him lay. The Indians won't bother him no more now."

That was all that was said about it. By now, the Indians had learned how deadly were the hunters' buffalo guns, even if there weren't very many of them. A few had crept up through the grass and up and down the stream-bed, staying out of sight until they were in rifle range. They were sniping now, so that a man didn't even dare raise his head. I don't know how many were hidden out there, but bullets came, at one time or another, from at least fifteen different spots.

A youngster named Billy Tyler and an older man named Fred Leonard suddenly ran from Myers' store and dodged around it toward the corral at the rear. I guess they wanted to make sure the gate was securely closed. Although, why that mattered to them, I can't imagine. Nobody here was going anyplace. We were under siege, and horses weren't any use to us.

They never reached the corral gate. All the Indians hidden along the creek suddenly opened fire on them, and when dust started kicking up in front of them and chips started flying out of the corral poles, they turned and streaked back toward Myers' store again.

They made it, but at the door of Myers' store Billy Tyler stopped and raised his rifle for a shot at one of those who had driven him and Leonard back. I saw him twitch and I knew he was hit even though he made no sound. Behind me, Masterson said, "Oh Christ! He's hit!" He got up and, as if there wasn't an Indian for a thousand miles, ran for Myers' store.

Dixon said, "Them two are good friends." Masterson made it to the door of Myers' store without being hit and disappeared inside.

Now there was a lull in the shooting, since all the post's defenders were keeping out of sight. The silence, after all that noise, was eerie. From Myers' store I could hear Billy Tyler groaning. It almost sounded like crying and maybe it was. After a while I heard him asking for water and I heard someone tell him there wasn't any. But pretty soon old man Keeler came shambling out of the store with a bucket in his hand. Dodging back and forth to throw off the Indians' aim, he headed for the corral.

His dog came running after him. Down along the creek those damn hideout Indians began to shoot again, only this time we all knew what to do. I'd gained enough strength back by now so that I could shove my Sharps out ahead of me and do my share of it.

Every time we'd see a puff of smoke we'd open up on it. So many bullets were hitting down there that after a minute or so no Indian dared to raise his head.

Old man Keeler got to the corral. He opened the gate and went in. He was standing still and a good target while he pumped the bucket full, but while the pump was squeaking we were firing just as fast as we could at the snipers along the creek.

Pretty soon the pump stopped squeaking and I heard the bar of the corral gate slammed home. The shooting went on, but old man Keeler came from behind Myers' store and headed for the door.

He reached it, too. And as soon as he did, we all stopped firing. Doing that was a mistake, as it turned out. The snipers down at the creek, cheated of their human target, now concentrated their fire on Keeler's dog.

The dog came around the corner of the store and headed for the door.

The first bullet knocked him flat. He began to yelp and to crawl toward the door. Immediately, we all opened up again, trying to make the Indians pull down their heads, but it was too late. A second Indian bullet stopped the dog and he lay there whining, unable to move because of a shattered spine, but wagging the tip of his tail and looking toward the door of Myers' store.

I saw Keeler trying to get out of it, and I saw several men yank him back. The dog twitched as another bullet hit, and another, and now he wasn't moving any more, just laying there in the dust, facing toward the place he had seen his master last.

The Indians weren't satisfied. We'd stopped shooting at them since there hadn't seemed to be any point in it now that the dog was dead. But they hadn't stopped. They kept firing, and their bullets kept thudding into the limp, dead body of the dog and the misses kept kicking up little geysers of dirt beside him and beyond.

Beside me, Dixon said, "Too bad. Old man Keeler put a heap of store by that old dog. Had him about ten or twelve years, I guess."

The Indians hadn't needed to kill the dog.

But then neither had O'Malley and Westerhoff needed to subject the Indian girl to the things they had. I guess hate picks its victims pretty impartially. Hatred thirsts for blood, and any blood will do.

Chapter 18

After the Indians killed the dog, the firing stopped altogether for a while. Only when one of the besieged defenders showed himself would the snipers down along the creek open up.

From where I lay, I could see Clinger's body. It lay in exactly the same position as when the man had gone down, so he was obviously dead.

I was glad I'd had no part in his death. I was interested in his wife. I wanted her. I wanted her to go with me to Dodge. I wanted to marry her. Hell, lots of people got married out here without knowing each other even as well as Edith Clinger and I knew each other.

And I'd been too long alone. I wanted a family. I wanted a home of my own and I wanted some little kids. I guess every man wants these things, but in some the need comes later than in others. Maybe the war had postponed my wanting them, but now I wanted them so bad it hurt when I thought about it.

Maybe she'd have tried going with me even if I'd been the one to kill her husband, but he'd have been there between us for a long, long time. Maybe he'd have stood between us forever and it would have made a successful marriage impossible.

I kept feeling better all the time. What had really floored me was the treatment of the wound in my leg, the whiskey being poured on it and the bandaging of it. Now that it was over with, the strength came back to me. Even though the leg still hurt as bad as it had before, it didn't make me feel so dizzy and so weak.

After those first two massed charges, there were no more, at least of that kind. Indians still charged in at regular intervals, parties of thirty or forty reckless young braves wanting to make a name for themselves and count coup upon an enemy. But they drew such a concentrated fire that soon even these attacks petered out.

Along about two in the afternoon, the women called to us from inside Rath's store, and we went in in shifts to eat. Jim Langston, Rath's clerk, volunteered to take food to Myers' store and to O'Keefe's. Everybody figured Hanrahan had enough food on hand to feed the men holed up there.

I watched Langston sprint toward Myers' store, bullets kicking up dust spurts behind him as he ran. One Indian bullet punctured the pail in which he was carrying hot stew, but otherwise he made it untouched. As soon as he dived into the door at Myers' store, I saw a man take the stew bucket from him and quickly stuff a finger into the bullet hole.

I heard my name called by Mrs. Olds, and eased myself back away from the piled-up grain sacks to the door of Rath's. I stood up as soon as I was inside and, using my Sharps fifty as a cane, I hobbled to the rear. After first making sure my gun was on half cock, I sat down at the bench.

Edith Clinger was watching me. When my glance met hers, she quickly looked away and a flush climbed into her face. She wants me the same as I want her, I thought. She'll go with me. The thought was sure an exciting one.

She brought me a plate of stew and a cup of hot coffee. I reached out and caught her hand, paying no mind to the other men sitting at the counter on both sides of me. I said, "I'm sorry."

"That he's dead? I don't really think you are. I think you should be relieved. He tried to kill you and he would have tried again.

Next time he might have hit you in a vital spot."

I let go her hand, but before she drew it away she gave my hand a little squeeze. I said, "All right. I guess I'm not sorry. Maybe what I meant to say was that I'm sorry you spent so much of your life trying to make your marriage with him work, only to have it end like this."

She said, "He died quickly and there was no suffering."

That seemed to be all there was to say on the subject of Clinger's death. And it suddenly struck me that in one way I was like him. Nobody would mourn me if I died today. I had no ties, no kin, nobody who gave a damn about me except, perhaps, Edith Clinger, and she scarcely knew me. I made my mind up that even if Edith wouldn't have me, it wasn't going to stay that way. Next year at this time there were going to be people who cared for me, who'd be sorry if I died. I intended to make sure there were.

I finished eating and went back outside. Dixon must have eaten and gone across to Hanrahan's because now he came running back, accompanied by Hanrahan. They dived, sliding behind the grain sacks while bullets from snipers along the creek kicked up dust behind them between Rath's and the saloon. Dixon panted, "They're out of ammunition at Hanrahan's. We come for more."

I said, "There's hot food in there, too, in case you haven't had any yet."

He said, "I ate, and there's cold meat and bread in the saloon." He went in. Hanrahan was grinning at me. He pulled a bottle of whiskey out from underneath his coat. "Lucky them redskinned devils didn't break this on the way over here."

I took the bottle from him, took a drink, and passed it along to the man next to me. I said, "Sure lucky that damn ridgepole cracked last night, wasn't it?"

He grinned back. "Sure as hell was. They'd a caught us sound asleep otherwise." He went into the store. After a few minutes he came out again, loaded down with ammunition, mostly rimfire cartridges for the big Sharps. But he also had some powder and ball and caps for smaller percussion guns. He and Dixon sprinted back toward the saloon, going suddenly and together, so that the snipers wouldn't be alerted by the first man to the second one.

By the time everybody had eaten, it was almost four o'clock in the afternoon. Some skulkers, among them the Indian bugler, came crawling out of the creek to go through the Shadler wagons over on the other side of the corral. I guess they thought they were safe because the corral stood between them and us. A few of the men opened up, though, shooting slowly and deliberately and aiming carefully between the poles of the corral whenever a target was visible. I heard the clang of a bullet on the bugle, and a man yelled exultantly, "Got that bugle-blowin' son-of-a-bitch! You see him go down? I bet there's a hole in that damn bugle big enough to stick your hand through!"

The other Indians ransacking the wagons gave it up immediately after the bugler was hit. They crawled back into the creek bottom and disappeared.

The sun sank slowly toward the horizon in the west. We'd have a respite as soon as it got dark, I thought, even though we wouldn't dare relax our vigilance. Indians don't like to fight at night. They have some superstition about the soul of a man killed at night never getting to the happy hunting grounds, instead he is left to wander around between heaven and earth forever. It didn't necessarily follow that every Indian believed that myth, any more than every white man believes in God or in the teachings of the

Bible. So there might be Indians coming in to see what they could steal or who they could kill without taking too much of a chance.

The bottle was passed back to me and I took another drink, this time a stiffer one than before. If I was going to get any sleep tonight, I'd have to load up on enough whiskey to kill the pain of my leg wound. Besides that, you couldn't hardly say I was completely recovered from the fight I'd had with Clinger.

In the first dusk, Masterson and another man I didn't know came running back to Rath's from the saloon. Masterson said, "We're going down to the creek soon's it gets dark and see if we can't get us some of those damn snipers that have been hiding there all day. They'll be skeedaddlin' as soon as they figure it's dark enough."

He didn't have any trouble getting volunteers to go with him. I'd have gone myself, but they didn't need somebody that had to hobble along using his rifle for a crutch. Soon as they had half a dozen men, they set out, crawling along the ground in the deepening dusk.

Edith Clinger came out of Rath's. I wanted to talk to her alone, so I pushed myself to my feet. I said, "It's dark enough to move around. Let's go over by the corral."

"All right." She positioned herself on the side where my wounded leg was and I put a hand on her shoulder so I wouldn't have to use my rifle for a crutch.

I don't know how a woman out in this God-forsaken place could manage to smell as good as she did. We reached the corral and stopped. I kept my hand on her shoulder even though I could have taken it away and used the corral poles for support. I said, "What are you going to do?"

She didn't pretend to misunderstand, but she didn't answer the question immediately. Instead she asked, "Do you think we are going to get out of this alive?"

That question kind of took me by surprise. I guess I hadn't even considered the possibility that the Indians would overrun this little settlement and kill us all. I said, "We'll get out of it all right. We got enough food here to last for months and we got enough ammunition to kill ten times that many Indians."

"What if they attack at night?"

"Well, I just hope nobody gives them that idea. Because if they'd attack at night the way they did this morning, they'd kill every man here in less time than it takes to tell about it. But they won't attack at night. Indians never do."

"I hope they know that," she said. Glancing at her face, I thought I saw a smile on it.

Down along the creek there was suddenly a flurry of shooting. After a little bit the half dozen men came back. One of them — Masterson, I guessed from his size — was dragging a dead Indian. He dragged him inside Myers' store and a few moments later I heard someone yell, "Hey, that's Stone Calf's kid!"

I didn't know who Stone Calf was, but guessing from the tone of the man's voice, he was well known, and that meant he was some kind of chief.

I looked down at Edith's face in the last of the dying light. I repeated, "What are you going to do?"

She said, "I will work here for the Olds as long as there is a job for me. When it's over, I suppose I will go to Dodge. I can probably get someone to buy the ranch. I'll write to Mr. Butterworth on Plum Creek and ask him to handle it for me."

I said, "I'm goin' to Dodge. I'm not goin' to stay and hunt buffalo." I tried to say it, but I couldn't seem to find the words. I wanted to ask her to marry me as soon as we got to someplace where there was a preacher, but to save my life I couldn't get the words out of my mouth. I guess maybe I was scared she'd turn me down. She was a pretty woman, and I wasn't much.

She said softly, "I've got to do something about Mr. Clinger's body. We can't just leave it there."

I said, "I'll walk you back to Rath's. Then I'll get some men and we'll go bury him."

She said, "You are a very kind man, Mr. Burdett." There was a touch of stiffness in her voice and I told myself I'd been a fool for not asking her. There were plenty of men here at this post that would jump at the chance to marry her, and maybe one of them would ask and get accepted before I ever got around to it. It was almost too late, but not quite. I said, "Ma'am, I got something to say to you, but I reckon it ought to wait at least until your husband is in the ground."

I was putting my weight on her shoulder and there was a change in the way it felt. I couldn't have said whether she tightened up or relaxed, but there *was* a change. She said, "I knew you did, Mr. Burdett. Thank you for waiting."

I said, "You *could* call me Jess."

"And you could call me something besides ma'am."

"Sure. Sure I will." We had reached Rath's

store. She went in. There were several men resting behind the piled-up grain sacks, some smoking, some not. I said, "Would a couple of you help me bury Mrs. Clinger's husband?"

Three men stood up. One said, "I'll get a shovel inside the store." He went in and came back a few minutes later. Everybody took their guns.

I remembered the exact spot where Clinger had been felled. I knew I could find it, even in the dark. I hobbled toward it.

Nobody hurried because we knew we had all night. Besides that, Clinger wasn't going to get the same kind of grave that Wallace and Dudley, Holmes and Blue Billy had. Clinger had been too thoroughly disliked.

We reached what I thought was the spot. Someone said, "He ain't here."

I said, "He's got to be here. We just ain't got the right spot, that's all."

Someone else said, "Spread out a little an' look around. We just got the wrong place in the dark."

The men scattered and wandered around aimlessly for several moments. Finally one of them came back. "He just ain't here. He's gone."

I asked, "How the hell could he be gone? The Indians wouldn't have any use for him except to take his scalp. They wouldn't have to drag his body off for that."

"Well, I don't give a damn what you say, he's gone."

However much I hated it, I had to admit the man was right. Clinger's body was gone.

This opened up a possibility I hadn't considered before. Since the Indians wouldn't have taken Clinger's body, then the man must still be alive. The blow of the tomahawk must have only knocked him out. He'd lain there all day, maybe conscious, maybe not.

When dark came, he probably crawled away. And if he was strong enough to crawl away, he was strong enough to try killing me again.

Uneasily I looked around, a little chill growing at the base of my spine. One of the men said, "That bastard is alive. We'd better get on back before he tries to bushwhack you." And we headed back toward Rath's, this time hurrying.

Chapter 19

I slept solidly that night, weakened by my wound, and never even felt the pain. The quarter bottle of whiskey I consumed before crawling into my blankets likely helped. At any rate, it was gray dawn when I awoke. Hagerman was squatting beside me, his two big Sharps lying at his side along with a pile of fifty to a hundred cartridges.

I sat up, wincing when I moved the leg. He looked at me. "How do you feel?"

"All right."

"Hell to get shot by a white man in an Indian fight."

It was a little early in the morning for humor, but I said, "Maybe I'll be luckier next time." I glanced out across the meadow. No Indians were in sight. I asked, "Think they'll come in like they did yesterday?"

"I hope the sons-a-bitches do. I'm ready for 'em."

I wondered when the man was going to be satisfied. Maybe never. He'd made a career of killing off the Indians' food supply. He'd certainly killed his share of Indians. He'd avenged his wife a dozen times over, but he wasn't satisfied and he probably would never be, not until he was dead.

The light strengthened and color tipped the scattered clouds overhead. Hagerman said, "Damn!"

So far, not even any snipers had opened up from the high grass and willows down along the creek. Suddenly Hagerman stood up. He gathered his cartridges and then picked up both rifles and the tripod. He grumbled, "If the bastards won't come to me, then, by God, I'll go to them."

He tramped out toward the creek. I didn't see any use in yelling at him because it wasn't going to do any good. Someone yelled to ask where the hell he was going, but he did not reply. He waded across the creek and walked out into the middle of the meadow. He acted as if there wasn't an Indian for a hundred miles.

Short of the fringe of brush and timber that ringed the meadow by a little more than an average rifle shot, he stopped. He squatted down and set his tripod up.

Masterson came out of the saloon. He walked over to where I was and stared out at Hagerman. "What the hell does he think he's doing?" he asked.

I said, "He's settin' up a stand."

"A stand? There ain't no buffalo within a dozen miles."

"A stand for Indians."

"Well, I'll he damned!"

Others were watching Hagerman now. Several yelled at him to come back, and not to be a fool. He didn't even look around.

He was ready now. His cartridges were in a pile beside him. His tripod was in place and both Sharps fifties were close at hand. But no Indians appeared.

He waited for what seemed about fifteen minutes. Then he stood up. He yelled derisively toward the fringe of trees and brush. He began to make obscene gestures toward the unseen Indians.

Finally, rifle smoke blossomed in the trees. Another rifle cracked. Pretty soon a dozen or more of them were firing.

Hagerman did a little dance, continuing the obscene gestures. He was taunting them and sooner or later his taunting would pay off. Then he'd get what he wanted, plenty of Indians to kill and, at the end, death for himself.

The man was demented, of course. He may also have been a fool. But it suddenly struck me that there was also a kind of magnificence in what he was doing. He seemed utterly without fear. He hated the Indians and this was his final demonstration of that hatred. Wherever his wife was, if she could see him now, she must have felt an intense pride, realizing that he had loved her enough to do this for her.

The sun was up now. And suddenly out of the fringe of brush and trees a line of mounted Indians swept. They had taken Hagerman's bait. They knew they could not kill him from concealment because he had deliberately set up his stand out of effective rifle range.

His taunts had gotten to them finally. Knowing many of them were going to die in the charge they made, they made it, nevertheless, in preference to taking his abuse any longer.

There must have been a couple of hundred at the very least. Not as many as had attacked the settlement yesterday, but more than enough, even for Hagerman. But he waited. He waited until they were less than two hundred yards away before he began firing.

Here at Rath's, over at Myers', and at Hanrahan's saloon, there was not a sound. Edith Clinger and Mr. and Mrs. Olds came out of Rath's to watch. It was hopeless and the end was predictable, yet it was magnificent, and it made a chill run up my spine.

Hagerman began firing, reloading rapidly and methodically. When one gun got too hot, he switched to the other one.

I say methodically, but by that I don't mean slowly. The shots came in rapid succession, deep and booming the way the report of a Sharps fifty is. With almost every shot an Indian tumbled out of his saddle and lay still on the ground. I kept no count and I doubt if anyone else did. We were too fascinated by the sight. Closer and closer the Indians came, and at a hundred yards they also began firing. Not a bullet touched Hagerman. Maybe he was lucky. More probably the Indians were simply unable to shoot accurately from the backs of their galloping mounts.

A few on the wings of the line, losing their courage, veered away. But the center, perhaps containing the fiercest of the Comanche fighters, came on, and on, even though by now they were dropping regularly.

Fifty yards. Twenty-five. Now Hagerman gave up the two Sharps and stood up, his revolver in his hand. It cracked, puny and insignificant compared to the Sharps, but almost as deadly.

They'd have liked to take him prisoner.

But too many of them had died, and he was still like a coiled rattler, fangs bared, capable of taking half a dozen more with him before they could take him prisoner.

They settled for killing him. Suddenly, hit for the first time, he jerked, and jerked again, and went to his knees. But his revolver was still up, and he was still pulling the trigger, even though the cylinder was empty now.

They surrounded him and finished him, and then, without dismounting or touching him, they galloped back into the fringe of trees, gathering up their dead and the loose horses as they went. Twenty minutes after it had begun it was over, and the meadow was empty again, empty except for Hagerman lying there, his thirst for vengeance satisfied at last.

Bat Masterson said, "Jesus Christ, I never seen anything like that in my life."

Billy Dixon said, "Come on. Let's go get him while we got a chance."

Half a dozen of them ran out into the meadow, splashing across the creek. They lifted Hagerman and brought him back, and behind them was one man carrying the two Sharps rifles which the Indians hadn't even bothered to steal.

They laid Hagerman down in front of

Rath's. He had not been touched. They had not scalped him, nor had they mutilated him in any way. This was the measure of their respect for one with such great courage, for one whose hatred exceeded even their own.

Mrs. Olds brought a blanket from Rath's, a new one, and laid it over him. And then, suddenly, I remembered Clinger.

There was a good chance that he had died, but I didn't dare rely on it. There was an equal chance that he was hid out someplace, like a dog who has crawled away to die. Only Clinger, even in his dying, was dangerous. Like Hagerman, he only wanted to kill, but in his case it was not Indians he wanted to kill. It was me.

But he didn't show himself throughout the day. By nightfall I was beginning to think he had really died. Yet if he had, where was his body? Why had it not been found?

The day had been quiet. The Indians had rarely showed themselves. Once in a while, one had ridden out as close as he dared and made contemptuous and obscene gestures at us. Each time it had happened, those who fancied themselves the best shots had banged away, trying to kill the reckless ones. In mid-afternoon one had been killed, and after that the Indians respected the range of the big Sharps buffalo guns and the skill of the men using them.

All through the night the hide hunters and skinners arrived at the settlement, singly and by twos and threes from their camps a dozen or more miles away. Most of them had been attacked in their camps. Few had any idea that Adobe Walls was under mass attack. But having been attacked, and being watchful because of it, they made it, in most cases, successfully through the Indians surrounding us.

That night, also, Henry Lease, riding the best horse left in the corral, headed out for Dodge to bring a rescue force to our aid. He led the animal out of the settlement, the horse's hoofs muffled with rags tied over them, and Lease's hand close to his nostrils so that he could quickly muffle any sound the horse might make. No one had any way of knowing whether he made it through or not, but we heard no uproar from the Indians, so chances were he did.

I dozed behind the grain sacks in front of Rath's store. Sometime during the late evening Edith Clinger came out carrying two water pails. She headed for the corral.

My leg didn't feel strong enough for carrying water, but I got up and followed her, limping painfully because of the stiffness in my leg. I wanted to talk to her for a while before she went back inside.

I heard the corral gate squeak, and heard the few horses inside spook away from her. I heard the sound of the pump, and the sound of water gushing from the spout into one bucket and then into the second. I moved toward the corral gate to intercept her there.

The pump stopped squeaking. I saw her dim shape coming toward me and opened my mouth to call to her so that seeing me suddenly wouldn't frighten her. But I never uttered a sound. Two shadowy shapes darted in, leaving the gate slightly ajar. They closed with her and the buckets clattered to the ground. She made a small and startled sound, but she got no chance to scream because a hand clamped itself over her mouth.

I had left my buffalo gun behind. Thank God, I still had the revolver in the holster at my waist. I drew it and thumbed the hammer back.

They heard that and whirled to face me, thrusting her in front of them.

There was an overcast covering the moon and stars. Only a small amount of light came through. Not enough to see my sights. Hardly enough to distinguish between Edith and the two Comanches who had captured her.

For what seemed an eternity, we stood there facing each other, motionless. They had to come through the corral gate, but I stood squarely in the opening, blocking it. I couldn't shoot and they knew it. And I didn't know but what there were others in the darkness behind me, perhaps even now readying themselves to leap.

Chapter 20

I suppose we only stood there for a few seconds. It seemed like hours. Edith must have been so terrified that she couldn't make a sound.

Not so the Indians. One of them must have spent a lot of time hanging around some Army post because he knew enough English to taunt me with, "White man! You know what we do to white squaw? Same thing you do to Indian squaw. We stake her out on ground. Many braves use her."

Suddenly I had a vision of that naked, abused, frightened Indian girl in O'Malley's wagon. And I guess I lost my head.

Hell, they were going to kill me anyway. Them or others in the darkness behind me. They could shoot and I couldn't. The only reason they hadn't already killed me was that the light was bad and they wanted to taunt me before they did finish me.

I shoved my gun back in its holster and made a run at them. They tried to get out of the way, but they had hold of Edith and they couldn't do it quickly enough. I hit all three and brought them tumbling to the ground inside the corral. Down in the dry manure that littered the corral, I drew my gun again and slashed at one of them with its barrel.

It grazed his head and stunned him, but he locked his arms around my legs, giving the other time to pick up Edith as if she had been a child and sprint for the corral gate.

He reached it and went through it. There was only one thing I could do. I shoved the revolver muzzle against the head of the Indian who was holding me and pulled the trigger. His grip relaxed and I clawed to my feet and hobbled toward the corral gate.

Edith was fighting now. Maybe her fright had been more for me than for herself, but there was sure as hell nothing holding her back right now. She was clawing and kicking and biting. The Indian was trying to throw her over the back of his horse while the other horse spooked away, frightened, reins trailing on the ground. Exasperated, the Comanche finally hit her a blow that knocked her sprawling. He turned to face me, gun in hand. There wasn't time for me to duck or swerve. I was committed to rushing him and I hadn't expected to have a chance to shoot.

But the shot that came did not come from the Indian's gun. It came from behind me, roaring out into the darkness of the night.

Something like a red-hot iron slammed into my back. Its force drove me forward and I fell, my face skidding in the dirt. The Indian fired, but his shot had been aimed at me, not at the unseen someone in back of me.

It never occurred to me that the one who'd hit me hadn't been shooting at the Indian. The brave gave up on Edith, who still lay stunned on the ground, and vaulted to his pony's back. He thundered away into the night, the loose pony of the dead Indian following.

I was hit, and hurt, but I wasn't out. I was conscious, and the pain that would set in later still had not come. My back, near my left shoulder where the bullet had hit, was only numb.

I had lost my revolver in the fall. I groped around for it without any particular urgency because I still thought that shot had hit me by mistake. But when I glanced back and saw a figure move on top of one of the hide wagons that had belonged to the dead Shadler brothers, I knew I had been wrong. Clinger was the one who had shot me. And now he was climbing down to finish me.

For an instant he was invisible to me as he jumped from the wagon and was hidden in its shadow. I groped frantically for the gun.

Edith, who must also have seen his silhouette against the sky, now came crawling toward me. I guess crawling wasn't exactly the word. Scrambling might have described it better, because she was moving fast, as if both our lives depended on it. I didn't know it at the time, but she had seen a glint of moonlight on my fallen revolver and knew where it was.

I was ten feet away from it. She reached it as Clinger came lumbering around the end of the corral, a big buffalo gun in his hands. He was still fifty feet away when Edith reached my gun. She didn't take time to try and throw it to me. There wasn't that kind of time. I heard the hammer click back, and dimly in the near-darkness I saw her raise the gun, holding it with both hands. She screamed, "Jake! Stop or I'll shoot!"

All she got out of him was a contemptuous snort. He came on and passed her as if she wasn't even there. Standing almost next to her, he raised the buffalo gun to take aim at me.

I knew if she couldn't muster what it took to fire, I was dead. At this range Clinger couldn't miss. Nor would he be stopped. Our gunfire had roused some of the men, but they were only now straggling out of the buildings to see what was going on. Before any of them reached us, I'd be dead.

Edith screamed once more, "Jake! Don't make me do it!"

He didn't even turn his head. The big hammer on the Sharps clicked back. I waited for the heavy slug to slam into me.

A gun blasted, but it wasn't the Sharps. It was the sharper crack of my own revolver and the flash came from where Edith was.

Clinger took a step, as if he'd lost his balance. He stood there for several moments, swaying like a tree that is undercut. The Sharps blasted, but it was reflex that pulled the trigger and the bullet missed.

He took another step, and then he fell. And suddenly men were all around us and I heard the voice of Mrs. Olds, and hands were helping me up and helping me back toward the light in the door of Rath's store.

Well, all the rest is history. Relief parties headed for Adobe Walls from both Dodge City and Fort Leavenworth. But the Indians had made their point.

Hanrahan, the only one still remaining of the post's founders, decided to abandon it. A great wagon train trailed north with the remaining trade goods and hides. And hardly was the caravan out of sight before the Indians moved in to burn the place.

As for Edith Clinger and myself, we went

north with the wagon train. We stayed in Dodge for a couple of months while my wounds healed. We finally rode out one day, after having been married by the Methodist preacher there in Dodge. We headed for that little ranch down south of the Canadian. Wasn't no good to her alone. She needed a man to run the place.

That was a long, long time ago. Now we have a ranch house with fifteen rooms. We have five sons and two daughters, mostly grown, and there's between ten and twelve thousand cattle roaming the north Texas plain with our brand on 'em.

But neither Edith nor I have forgotten. Sometimes we still remember those days at Adobe Walls. And sometimes Edith still cries out in the night, dreaming that the Indians have got hold of her. When that happens, she turns to me and I hold her until her trembling has quieted.